Sitting on the Porch with Jesus

Sitting on the Porch with Jesus

Rob Strauss

Sitting on the Porch with Jesus

© Rob Strauss 2018

This book is a work of fiction. Named locations are used fictitiously, and characters and incidents are the product of the author's imagination. Any resemblance to actual events or places or persons, living or dead, is entirely coincidental.

Published by
Lighthouse Christian Publishing
SAN 257-4330
5531 Dufferin Drive
Savage, Minnesota, 55378
United States of America

www.lighthousechristianpublishing.com

Introduction

All Bible references in the text are from the New International Version (NIV) unless otherwise noted. Other references, when known, are noted in the text.

There are times when I have Jesus quoting from the New Testament, and I still use quotation marks and double-quotation marks as usual when quoting from the Bible. This might seem strange when I show Jesus quoting himself from a certain passage, but I decided to keep the convention to avoid confusion.

I use an uppercase pronoun for God, but I did not maintain this convention when referring to Jesus in the third person. It would have made me crazy trying to keep the capitalization straight. This doesn't detract, however, from the esteem and respect I hold for Jesus. With other words, such as "Truth" and "Savior," I have capitalized when I felt it was appropriate.

This was originally intended as a private journal, which I expanded and fictionalized where appropriate. The stories and the personalities are true, but this is a fictionalized account of my experiences and conversations.

I have provided a "Notes and Acknowledgment" section at the end for those who which to delve deeper into the topics discussed.

Contents

Prologue:

At the start of the year I became a statistic: one of the "unemployed." It wasn't the first time, not even the second or third time. But I sure hoped it was the last time.

While I did worry through those previous bouts of unemployment, this time seemed different. For one thing, I was older. At this point in my life all I expected to worry about professionally was how my employer was going to get by without me when I retired. For some reason I hadn't expected to be running around—virtually if not literally— peddling my resume and looking for a yet another job.

Call me a traditionalist, but all I expected out of life, career-wise, was to be employed by some company for 30 or more years and retire with a pension, as my father did and his father before him. Was that too much to expect? Apparently, yes it was. Someone forgot to inform the <u>economy</u> of my expectations. It just didn't receive the memo.

Having been through this several times over the past two decades I fell back into my previous between-job habits. I updated and brushed-up my resume, modernizing it from the last spasm of job-seeking (resume styles change as often as lady's hemlines), and re-initiated my old queries on the online employment services. In the past this activity was much more labor-intensive: perusing local newspapers, searching the want-ads and getting newsprint all over your hands and even on your nose (those classified ad fonts are pretty small), then typing cover letters to go with your professionally-printed resumes and mailing them out via "snail-mail." And of course the wait. That part hasn't changed much over the years, even with all this technology.

Also as part of my habit when I'm unemployed, I <u>prayed</u> about it. I was always taught that if something was on my mind, if something was pressing heavily on my soul and wouldn't let up, I should "take it to the Lord." I always did, and I always will. I laid my problems at the feet of Jesus, and sought power through Christ, who gives me strength (Philippians 4:13 - "I can do all things in Christ, Who strengthens me"). And that should have been enough.

But it wasn't.

This time was different.

This time I was scared.

Really scared.

I guess I hadn't realized how scared I was until my wife came home one night crying. She had tried to hide her tears, but I noticed immediately. "What's wrong," I asked. I thought it had something to do with her job.

"I'm scared," she said through the watery eyes.

"Of what?"

"Of what's going to become of us…"

You can imagine how this made me feel. As a traditionalist I have this unrealistic notion I should be the so called "bread-winner" of the family. The men of my generation, while we totally recognize the equality of the opposite sex, still have this entrenched need to "bring home the bacon," to be the "primary earner." It's what most men would say is a "pride thing." I will admit it right now: this is an unreasonable and outmoded idea, and shouldn't be part of the male psyche. But it still is part of the male psyche, at least in a high percentage of males. And I'm one of them.

For my own part, I could do without male pride, thank you very much. It's nothing but trouble and only gets in the way. And when it rears its ugly head it can be quite irksome.

Now I was scared myself. What was to become of us? I'd been looking for a job for a few months, with very little to show for it. Unemployment was up to ten percent and the economy, as I said before, was not cooperating. My prayers started to take on a desperate tone. I was begging God to get me a job. But nothing was happening. No one was calling for interviews; no one was beating down my door to hire me. Even my old recruiter contacts were unusually quiet. My faith began to wane. This was a crisis. I was losing touch with myself and who I was. I was losing touch with God. I had to do something.

So I went shopping. For a chair.

A rocking chair.

A special rocking chair. One for my porch. One for Jesus.

Some time ago I received a tip on praying from an old deacon friend of mine. I had always had a problem with praying, especially out loud. I was raised a Catholic and taught mostly memorized prayers from the catechism. When I became an adult and tried "extemporaneous" prayer I was miserable at it. I felt I needed the security of the memorized text; I wasn't comfortable talking to God in my fumbling, stuttering manner. Of course a friend pointed out that Moses himself had a speech impediment of sorts (Exodus 4:10 – "Then Moses said to the Lord, "Please, Lord, I have never been eloquent, neither recently nor in time past, nor since. You have spoken to your servant; for I am slow of speech and slow of tongue.") But it didn't help. I wasn't slow of tongue (quite the opposite); I was slow of mind. I could never organize my thoughts into the right words to make a good prayer.

My friend suggested I try getting a chair for Jesus. Just any chair, but it helps if you feel it's special. Put the chair where you like to sit, maybe on the porch or in the den...someplace quiet, where you would normally talk to a friend. Then just sit and imagine Jesus sitting in that other chair...and simply <u>talk</u> to him. Talk to him as you would to a good friend or close family member. Closer if you can. Open up to him. If you can imagine Jesus sitting in the chair, listening, offering suggestions, you don't feel the pressure of forming complete sentences or concrete thought constructions. You're don't feel as if you're praying to God, although you are, actually; you're just talking to a friend. A close friend. The closest, really.

So I went to the Good Will store and purchased a second-hand rocking chair and put it on my porch where I like to sit in the morning. And I began to talk to Jesus.

Chapter One: The Unemployed Guy

"Good morning Jesus."

"Good mornin' Rob." Jesus answered, smiling and rocking comfortably in the chair I had gotten for him. "How are you today?"

"Well, to tell you the truth, I'm pretty worried. I've been unemployed for months, and the unemployment checks will stop in a couple of weeks. I really don't know what Lucy and I will do if I don't find a job."

Jesus rocked a bit more in the chair. He seemed to be pondering. "Well, I can understand you being worried. It's only natural. Anyone else in your place would be worried." Then he looked at me and smiled again; I could tell he wanted me to add something.

I knew what he wanted me to say.

"But I'm not just <u>any</u> person, is that what you're saying?"

"Well, <u>you</u> said it."

"Wasn't that the same response you gave when they asked if you were the Son of God?"

"Was it?" he said, feigning ignorance. "Well, if something works, you stick with it!"

I knew what he was getting at, but I was avoiding it in my own mind. You know, as when you face a difficult job and you consciously or unconsciously procrastinate against doing it, always finding ways to dodge it. Well, that's what I was doing in my mind. I knew what Jesus meant. He meant that when I became a Christian, I became a <u>new</u> man. I'm not just <u>any</u> guy now; I live in the grace of our Lord Jesus Christ. My life should be a celebration of the glory of the Lord. When life hands me lemons I'm supposed to make lemonade. I should have faith that my life will go in the direction God wants. But it's oh-so-hard to be a good Christian when things go wrong.

I guess I should take inspiration from Paul. All sorts of bad things happened to him, but he glorified in his suffering because he knew that God's grace and power were magnified when he persevered over adversity. Jesus told Paul: "My grace is sufficient for you, for my power is made perfect in weakness." (2 Cor 12:9). So when things go wrong I know I should look to Paul as a source of strength.

"Although I know, in my heart," I said to Jesus, "that God will make everything all right in the end, and I shouldn't worry because I have His rod and staff to comfort me…it's just not easy to put that into practice in the <u>real</u> world."

Jesus smiled. "I love it when you say things like '…in the <u>real</u> world.' What, do you think? The apostles and I lived in some make-believe world?"

"No, of course not," I said.

"Yet," he went on, "you mentally compare the life described in the Bible to the way things are in your 'real world' and then you decide that old stuff is just too hard to actually do in your world. But in many ways my disciples and I were living in a world more real than the one you live in now."

I was vigorously shaking my head. "No, that's not it at all. I know times were tough for you and the apostles and everybody back in Bible times, it's just…there're so many other things to worry about in today's world, so many new things that didn't exist back in your time, and it makes life these days very difficult to handle, especially emotionally. Now stop that!" He was mimicking playing a violin with his arms.

"You're making me cry," he said while continuing to stroke the imaginary violin.

"I didn't think you would resort to modern sarcasm…"

"Hey, whatever works!" He finished the imaginary piece he was playing on his invisible violin. "Sorry, I couldn't resist." He smiled warmly at me. "Rob, I know, if you think about it for a minute, you'll see that each generation's problems are unique but not new. When Peter and James and I traveled on the road we had to be careful of bandits and highway men. You could lose your life if you were not careful. Nowadays you don't have to be watchful of bandits, but you still might be killed on the highway going 65 miles an hour in a car. The dangers are different but just as deadly. And the same goes for all the countless problems you say you have in these times. They're a little more sophisticated, but in the long run they're the same. Each generation brings its own problems. You don't want me to go into the 'Sermon on the Mount' again, do you?"

"I know," I said. "Chapter six from Matthew: 'Consider the lilies of the field...' and all that. I know what you're getting at. But I can't seem to make my faith work in that way. When I'm out of a job, there's still the worry and the stress and the aggravation.... I can't seem to stop worrying about tomorrow, and the next day, and the day after that."

Jesus nodded. "Hmm. Yes, I can tell you're sincere in what you're saying. What should I do to show you I'm still in charge? How can I convince you that you don't need to worry? Why don't you just look to me, and leave it to me? What else do you need?"

Okay, so there it was. The King of Kings was asking me: What do you need? You don't respond to that question flippantly. But I honestly could not come up with a true answer to his question without being factious. It was my typical defensive response.

"You mean besides a miracle?" I regretted the words as soon as I said them.

Jesus gave me that <u>look</u>. You know...the look you get from someone when they know you're not giving the question enough thought. "My words were enough for the people on that hilltop, why do you seem to need more?"

I was struggling to vocalize what had been knocking around in my head for weeks. I think my problem was that there were just too many things to worry about. I didn't have a job, and the bills were piling up... It was overwhelming.

"I think," I finally managed to say, "that the problem is that in those days people didn't have as much to worry about as we do today. I mean, back then, you were a peasant or something, you farmed the land... Sure, you didn't own the land, and you didn't get paid to work it, but at least you took away food from the land to feed your family. The landlord couldn't just let you die; he needed you to work the land. It wasn't equitable, but at least it was survival. And they didn't have to worry about unemployment and global warming or electric bills or Internet connections and all that. I mean, we've kind of grown-up in the past 2,000 years and technologically we're light-years ahead of civilization as it was in the old days."

Jesus sat there listening, thoughtfully taking in my words. He nodded, keeping his hands in his lap as he listened. "Okay, if I understand what you're saying," he began, "all those technologies, all those gadgets that were supposed to bring you comfort and easy living have actually brought anxiety and stress, right?" I nodded my head. "So you're saying that folks in the so-called 'Dark Ages' may have been oppressed and lived in abject poverty, but they had peace-of-mind often enough?" Again I nodded. "All right, you're basically correct. It's true, back in my day our most stressful thought was usually: 'Where will I get enough food for today?' while your minds are filled with a multitude of thoughts about when to pay the bills, how will I meet this or that deadline, why does my wife or husband seem so remote and distant? Should I lie on my tax returns? And on and on... So yes, there is a difference there. Things were emotionally simpler in the old days.

"But on the other hand," he continued, "your generation is spared all the worries about health and disease that afflicted most of the old world. You live longer, and you're relatively healthy most of the time. That is, if you're not poisoning yourselves with sugar, alcohol, nicotine or caffeine. But materially you have it quite good today. Poverty in the old days meant living in what you'd call today a shanty or a lean-to, with a dirt floor and no windows except a hole in the roof if you were lucky. You never knew where your next meal was coming from, and you never knew when death would come for you or your children; death was a constant companion back then. If you needed to get somewhere...you walked, unless you were lucky enough to have a horse or mule, but that was unlikely if you were a peasant. For warmth you burned wood if you could find it, and if it got too hot in the summer, well, you suffered. Or died.

"Today even the so-called poor live in relative luxury. There's state-provided housing with heat and perhaps even air conditioning, and sometimes even a state provided cell phone. There are food stamp programs and shelters in every city throughout this country, and many people considered to be on the 'poverty level' even have an automobile. For those who don't, there's public transportation."

I had to admit I hadn't considered any of that.

"So you think you'd like to trade in your problems of today for the problems of yesterday?" Jesus asked. "I'm not sure you could handle them. But then again, the folks of yester-year would have a hard time with the problems you people deal on a daily basis too."

He must have noticed my perplexed expression, so he clarified.

"What I'm getting at is: it's all relative. And if it's all relative, then you only have a subjective view of your problems, from your own stand-point. What you need is to rely on the objective view. But who has an objective view? Everybody is working from their own perspective. To have an objective view of today's problems you'd have to stand outside of the world. And who stands outside of the world?"

This is what's popularly called a "Duh Moment."

"Huh, you do?"

"Yes! My Father in Heaven," he amended. "I'm your envoy to Him. As you know, I have a certain bias toward you folks." He smiled and winked.

"So you're saying that if I rely on God I don't have to worry about my problems?"

"Well, worrying actually has a useful purpose, if you don't take it too far. My Father wouldn't have put it in us..." (Jesus noticed my arched eyebrows at the mention of "us" and smiled again). "Yeah, I'm including myself in there; I worried sometimes, but not about the things you worry about. Mostly over the apostles."

"So, what do you mean? Worry's like a defense mechanism?"

"That's not my department, but sure, something like that. When you worry, your brain is using that wonderful ability God gave all of us: the ability to plan ahead. Other creatures cannot do that; they live in the moment <u>only</u>. Now, that's not a bad thing, but again, it also has its disadvantages. If you can't imagine what's coming up next, you can't make arrangements to make sure future events turn out in your favor. That's how we plan, hunt, gather, build things, and do all that great stuff we do. But you're supposed to imagine <u>both</u> good and bad things happening in the future, not just the bad things. When you worry excessively your brain is imagining too many negative outcomes; you're having trouble imagining the positive results that have just as good a chance of happening as the bad ones. All I'm saying is: you need to even it out."

"Easier said than done I'm afraid, Jesus."

"Funny, that's what Peter said about walking on water…"

I laughed at that. Jesus could be funny when he wanted to. "Okay. So you can help me 'even it out'?"

"Hey, I'm your man! Mr. Super-even is my middle name."

"I thought it started with an 'H'?"

Chapter Two: The Stern Pastor

I received a call from the pastor of our church last night. Seems he had some legal documents he needed me to sign as chairman of the Building Committee, so I invited him over the next morning. I was sitting with Jesus out on the porch when Pastor drove up in his dilapidated old pick-up. Our pastor was something of an automotive hobbyist and loved working on old cars and trucks. The one he was driving today seemed in need of a bit more work though; it coughed and sputtered badly when he turned off the ignition, belching black smoke into the air.

"Get a horse!" I called to him as the truck struggled to come to rest. He got out of the truck and smiled, slamming the door behind him; the truck—finally giving up the ghost—shuttered into place.

"Good morning Rob!" he said stepping up to the porch holding a brown leather briefcase. "Got those papers I need you to sign right here." He placed the briefcase on the small wooden bench I kept on the porch and opened it, exposing a pile of very legal looking documents. I looked at the stack in amazement.

"That many? I didn't know there would be so many pages to sign."

"Yeah, I think we killed a few forests with this transaction. Why?" he asked as he handed me his pen from his coat pocket. "Afraid of getting writer's cramp?"

"Well, yeah," I said defensively as I took the pen. "Since I type most everything these days, my hands aren't used to writing with these primitive writing implements."

I noticed he was about to sit in the rocker I had purchased for Jesus, so I purposely steered him toward the three-legged stool next to my chair. "Better sit here Pastor...that chair is for Jesus, remember?"

I had spoken to Pastor about my idea of getting a chair for Jesus and talking to him as I would a special friend, but he had not warmed up to my idea as I had hoped he would. Our pastor was a strict theologian who frowned on my—as he put it—"disrespectful" attitude toward my Lord and Savior. We had discussed our difference on the matter, even to the point of him strongly suggesting I give up the idea and return to regular prayer and the study of the scriptures, but I disagreed. Not about studying the scripture; I did that all the time as a follower of Christ. But I thought my form of prayer was just as suitable as Pastor's "acceptable" variety. I did not feel I was being disrespectful toward Jesus.

Pastor frowned as he sat in the stool. "Now Rob," he said patiently, "you know I disapprove of your cavalier attitude toward our Savior, right?"

"Yes Pastor," I murmured dutifully under my breath. "Are we going to get into that debate again?"

"Well, I'm your spiritual shepherd, and I'm supposed to offer you spiritual direction and guidance, so I'm only doing my job when I tell you that you're bordering on heresy by making Jesus into a 'buddy.'"

We had gotten into this conversation a few times after I had purchased the rocking chair, and I understood where he was coming from, academically. But I disagreed with him pragmatically; I felt what I was doing was bringing me closer to my Lord, and helping me to sort things out in my own mind.

"But I told you how I always had a problem with prayer," I countered uneasily. "This is helping me work things out with my Savior, not hindering. I need to see Jesus as a friend who I can talk to and ask questions. It doesn't diminish the respect I have for him or his Father."

"And that's great, Rob, it really is," Pastor said. "But don't you see the danger of thinking of your Lord and Savior as a buddy? You're emphasizing Jesus' 'niceness,' and as I told you, Jesus was not always so nice. There are some hard and difficult doctrines you have to accept to be a true Christian. Making our Savior into your buddy is pleasant, but what about sin? What about God's judgment? How do you reconcile the need for repentance and atonement with your buddy? How does holiness fit in with your pal?"

I always felt intimidated by the clergy, especially as a young boy. And Pastor, although a great guy and a good friend, was equally intimidating to me sometimes. Oh, he could joke and kid around with the best of 'em, but when it came to religion—when it came to salvation and your immortal soul—

well, he was all business then. He was a staunch and serious clergyman with a job to do: to keep his flock on the straight and narrow road of the Gospel. And he was basically saying that my attitude toward Jesus was non-Biblical and wrong. But I couldn't swallow that just now. I knew why I thought as I did, and I knew how good this "exercise" of talking to Jesus was for me, so I just couldn't give up and admit I was wrong.

"Pastor," I sighed, "I was raised in a strict Christian environment, and taught to be very respectful and reverential toward God. As a child I saw Him as an unapproachable monarch, the same way a peasant might see a king, just as many visualize God today: as a mighty king, with flowing robes and long, white beard. As for His son, Jesus…well, he was just as mysterious: the Son in the Holy Trinity, and equally unapproachable by mere mortals. Even the priests, who seemed to be closest to God, had to bow and murmur prayers constantly to the Lord of Heaven, who remained enigmatic and distant. For me it kept God and Jesus at arm's length, maybe farther. Approaching God was very formalized and scripted, and to do it properly you had to have an ordained minister of the church with you. It wasn't until I learned it was possible to have a personal relationship with my Savior that I started to feel closer to Jesus."

"Rob, having a personal relationship with Jesus is a good thing, but it can also be misleading; the word 'personal' can have many meanings. In Biblical times, unlike today, folks did not 'get to know' each other (Pastor made quote signs in the air as he said that) as friends do today. Back then a friend was someone who would look out for you and your interests, not someone you would sit down with to watch the game and have a few beers. They didn't define a 'friend' as we do today, and they would have no idea what we mean by 'personal relationship.' Plus, thinking of Jesus as your 'buddy' detracts from God's holiness. I don't want you to get the impression that Jesus is your 'homeboy' or anything like that. When you start talking to Jesus as a pal, as a buddy, it shows an absence of reverence, and this can lead to a lack of personal accountability that reduces spiritual growth. In your friendly conversations with Jesus I doubt you ever touch on sin or redemption, or any of the more unpleasant aspects of God's judgment."

"Actually," I added sheepishly, "we do touch on those topics sometimes."

"But probably not enough," Pastor quickly injected. "Rob, I know you want to think that you can talk to Jesus anytime, about anything that might be troubling you…and you can! But taken too far that can lead to the 'genie in a bottle' syndrome: thinking that God is only there for your wishes. Don't you see? When you do that you're highlighting yourself, not God. You're reducing the Lord to a self-help guru who is only interested in your self-fulfillment. The result of this self-focus makes it seem as if God is secondary to our own needs. But that is <u>incorrect</u>. Our purpose on this earth is to worship the Lord, not to fulfill our own agendas. When you go to church, you're not supposed to 'get something out of it'; God is supposed to 'get something out of it.' Worshipping God is not for you, it's for God. All I'm saying is you need to demonstrate a greater respect for God and His holiness, and less obsession with your own desires and self-fulfillment."

I knew that Pastor was not purposely scolding me, but his words hurt nonetheless. I looked over imploringly to where Jesus sat in his rocking chair, listening to our conversation.

"What are you looking at me for?" Jesus asked. "He's right."

I nodded. Essentially Pastor was right. But all that reverence and awe from my early years, the melodramatic veneration toward God that always seemed pretentious and a bit insincere…all that adulation and scripted praying just didn't do it for me; I could never feel close to God worshipping Him in that manner. And it didn't help me feel the joy I was supposed to feel at being a Christian. I knew a lot of people who felt the same. I often spoke with newcomers to our church, and many times they've told me that the thing they liked most was the sense of joy they felt. While we do take God's Word very seriously, we don't get hung up on the "churchiness" of our services or take ourselves too seriously. I always loved that about our church. Nevertheless our pastor is still a stern ecclesiastic, and he takes his role as spiritual overseer very seriously. While he might give a sermon about God's understanding and love he always added God's judgment and what we needed to do to repent and be saved. It was a serious business to him, as indeed it is to all of us. But Pastor, I felt, and the folks like him, took it to extremes.

"I understand what you're saying," I admitted, "but I don't agree that it's wrong to think of Jesus this way. After experiencing so much awe and trepidation in church as a kid, I really appreciate that the faith I adhered to now is more joy-based, with more emphasis on love and service to others, not on intricate liturgies and inflexible dogma. But don't get me wrong Pastor... I do respect Jesus, and I still hold him in the same awe...but not so much trepidation. No, I would say my childhood fear of God has matured now to a wonder, an incredible admiration...an adoration of Jesus and his Father. I just want to love and respect God and His son, love my neighbor...and, at the same time, not take myself too seriously, because that kind of seriousness, to me, inhibits love and joy."

I looked over to Jesus, and he was nodding slightly, as if not necessarily agreeing with me, but understanding my feelings anyway.

"Well," sighed Pastor, "let's just agree to disagree for now, shall we?" And sign the papers, will you! I can tell you're stalling!"

So I signed the papers...all of them...and Pastor said goodbye and left in a cloud of black smoke jettisoned by his pickup truck. As he drove off I had the urge to sit and talk with Jesus, but considering the conversation I just had with Pastor it seemed inappropriate.

But Jesus was not going to let me sulk off into a corner and mope. "So...don't you want to talk about this?" he asked as I was about to go back into the house. "I can see that the conversation with your pastor disturbed you."

I turned and plopped down in my chair. "Yeah, you're right," I said reluctantly. "It did disturb me. Now I have to question whether it's right to even be talking to you like this, considering what Pastor said. And I know he's essentially right... But what do _you_ think? Do you think I'm being disrespectful to you and your Father by talking to you like this, as if you were a good friend, and not God incarnate?"

Jesus hung his head low, apparently preparing to tell me something I was not going to like. Then he looked up. "Rob, I <u>am</u> a good friend. As I told the apostles: 'I no longer call you servants, because a servant does not know his master's business. Instead, I have called you friends, for everything that I learned from my Father I have made known to you.' (John 15:15) But your Pastor is absolutely right when he says there's a risk in thinking of me this way and talking to me this way. You must never forget to Whom you are speaking. But it's so easy to forget when we converse like this, sitting on the porch, just talking as friends. There's a tendency to 'dumb-down' God and to rationalize around difficult doctrine. I think that's what your pastor is afraid of."

"But I tried praying as I was taught in Sunday School, even with all the 'thees' and 'thous' put in…and it was fine, for what it was…but it seldom helped me with the big questions. And you remember when I lost my faith and was struggling with doubt a few years back…how I forced myself to talk to you every night…and how we both worked things out so I could have a stronger faith. I would never have become the Christian I am now if I couldn't have talked to you as a good friend back then…as a pal who understands. And even now—no, especially now—I really feel this time I spend with you on the porch has real spiritual value, not just for me but possibly for others as well. I just can't…I won't…give it up."

Jesus nodded. "I can see you feel strongly about this, and perhaps it's not as bad as you're imagining."

"What do you mean?"

"Well, I think the cause of this difficulty is three-fold actually," he said, "and the first two reasons have to do with culture."

"Culture?"

"Yes! You see, in this country you live in a democracy, not a monarchy. You don't really know what it's like to live under the rule of a monarch; you're not used to it. You're not familiar with the lingo and you don't know how it feels to have someone be the absolute ruler over you. Back in my day, in Asia and all over the world really, everyone lived under some form of absolute rule. Citizens did not elect their kings, they simply got a king…and were told in no uncertain terms that they had to fear and respect this king. In ancient times we knew what it meant to live under a monarchy, and we were familiar with being ruled absolutely by someone we did not select ourselves. That's where the difficulty lies. Much of the language in the Bible concerning God stems from this culture of monarchy. Back then people knew how to bow down to a king, so bowing down to God came naturally to them. You folks in this country value your freedom (it's almost a holy word), and bow down to no one. You're not familiar with having a king, so how would you know how to act around one?"

I was desperately trying to follow what Jesus was explaining. "So since we live in a democracy we don't know how to be respectful to God?"

Jesus shook his head. "Not exactly. You know <u>intellectually</u> how to be respectful, but you're not in the practice of doing it. You know rationally that it's right and proper to bow down to God, but in your culture you sometimes have a hard time doing it. In those countries where they're accustomed to having kings and queens, they bow and kneel with great alacrity because they know what it's all about. In this country it's unnatural; you're not in the habit of doing it, so you don't really understand it."

I found what Jesus was saying to be very interesting, but it didn't necessarily make me feel any better. "You mentioned there might be other causes?"

"Yes. The other problem, as I see it, is that the Bible describes the relationship people should have with the Lord as a kind of patron-client relationship, similar to the institution as it was practiced in the ancient Roman Empire. In my day we understood this; we were all very familiar with the practice of 'clientage': the institution of Roman patrons and their various clients. You know, back in the old Roman Empire regular people had no 'rights' as you understand them, such as the right to 'life, liberty and the pursuit of happiness.' Nope, if you wanted anything back then you had to know the right people, and that's where the Roman concept of the patron and the client came in. A patron was the guy with the connections, and his clients were the folks who needed things from him. Today you have the upper class, who in my day we called 'the rich,' and you have the lower class, 'the poor,' just as we did in my day. But you look at them differently than we did. Today you see the lower classes as folks who've simply haven't had as many opportunities as the upper classes, or as people who have made more mistakes than the upper class, but you still see them as essentially equal. Of course there was really no 'middle class' in my day unless you include the 'merchant class,' which was really just developing back then. But in the old days people were not considered equal. Far from it. The 'rich' parceled out goods and power to the 'poor'—the lower classes—through clients, so having a patron was essential back then if you were to prosper and succeed. It was an integral part of the culture. So you have language in the New Testament that uses this patron/client culture, and if you're not familiar with it, you don't understand it properly.

"For example," Jesus continued, "in John 16, verse 24b it says: 'Ask and you will receive, and your joy will be complete.' Now the Greek word for 'ask' that John uses in this text can mean 'demand' but it can also mean 'to plead, to beg.' In the patron/client culture in which this was written no one would interpret this to mean 'demand.' No one would ever think to 'demand' good things from God; a client will 'beg' or 'plead' for good things from his patron, and a patron will 'demand' things from his clients, but not the reverse. It was part of the culture. You in this culture are not as familiar with this state of affairs as we were back then, so you muddle through as best you can."

Some of what Jesus was saying was familiar to me; I remember reading about the practice of "clientage" in ancient Rome when I studied history in high school and college. But if he was suggesting that this excused my nonchalance with the Prince of Peace…well, that just didn't hold water. Sure we in this culture were not accustom to the patron/client institution of ancient Rome…but we were not entirely unfamiliar with it either. Just because something is not part of your culture doesn't mean you can't exercise some discipline when necessary.

"I appreciate how you're trying to help me feel better about this Jesus," I said, "but I don't think those reasons get me off the hook. I mean…just because I'm set in my ways and want to do things my way? No, I know there's a right way to do things…and there's a wrong way. I'm beginning to think the way I speak with you on the porch is the wrong way." I bowed my own head in frustration.

"Perhaps if we discuss the third reason for the problem as I see it you might feel better?" Jesus suggested.

"A third reason?" I raised my head slightly.

"Yes, the problem of language. Proper translation is always an issue when you're talking about words that were written down 2,000 years ago, and in another language…and a 'dead' language at that. For example the Hebrew word for 'fear' used in the Bible. There's actually two Hebrew words used for 'fear': <u>pahhad</u> and <u>yirah</u>. The word 'pahhad' literally means 'to shake' or 'to tremble' and the other words you would normally associate with the English word 'fear.' It's the instinctive, primal (what Freud called 'the Id') often irrational kind of fear we're all familiar with and associate with that word. For example, in Job 4:14 it says: 'Fear and trembling seized me and made all my bones shake.' In this case 'pahhad' (fear) is a noun, and it literally means 'being afraid'.

"'Yirah' on the other hand is the feeling you might get when you encounter something bigger and more magnificent than you're accustom to. You know, something way out of your comfort-range; something extraordinary in your experience. Essentially it means 'awe.' If you've ever felt the healing of a deep emptiness in your heart, or discovered something you only dreamed could be true…or even felt the glow of inspiration when you came to comprehend a wonderful truth…you will understand this feeling. It can involve what you call 'fear' but it's much more than that, and not a negative feeling at all. This is what the Bible means when it says in Deuteronomy 6:13: 'Fear the Lord your God, serve Him only and take your oaths in His name.'"

I was starting to take heart from what Jesus was saying. "And that verse from Proverbs…I think it's in the first chapter, where it says: 'The fear of the Lord is the beginning of knowledge'… Does that use the word 'yirah' as well?"

"Yes," Jesus said, smiling. "Chapter one, verse seven. And you will notice that it says it's the 'beginning of knowledge,' not the end. A proper respect and awe of the Almighty is always the best place to start to find wisdom, even in this world. But it's not the end. No, too many of my followers seem to confuse that, and they confuse what it is I truly desire of them."

"It's not fear?" I asked.

"Not as such, no," Jesus said. "Many believe they must live in fear of God's punishment, but that is not the best way. No, what my Father and I want and expect is a sense of 'yirah'…of awe…and not so much the trembling and shaking and all that. It's unproductive. And the sad thing is, those of my followers whose faith is 'fear' based—based on pahhad and not yirah—will have a difficult time experiencing the fruits of the Spirit, the love and joy and peace we all share. For many of them it will be as if they're under a dark cloud, fearful, uncertain…and this can lead to animosity toward God. They may come to even distrust God. Additionally, fearful Christians tend to stay away from sinners…and you know I don't want that. How else can you take the Good News to them? But fearful Christians will disassociate themselves from sinners, afraid they might be infected with sin. They don't participate in life because they're afraid they might engage in 'ungodly behavior' and be tempted by the ways of the world. They may become judgmental, and separate themselves from life and regular people. And worse yet…fearful Christians have a tendency to punish themselves for their own emotions and cravings. But while they're punishing themselves they are not loving their neighbor…and they're certainly not serving God. Their fear renders them useless to me."

"So you don't really want followers who live in fear?"

"Not that kind of fear, no. Even real fear, pahhad, can have different aspects. Often when the Bible speaks of 'fearing the Lord,' and the word pahhad is used, it's not talking about 'servile fear': the fear of getting into trouble. It's taking about 'filial fear': the fear, or concern, of offending someone you love. And as I keep reminding you Rob, the crux of it all is love, not fear. You cannot love something you fear. Fear destroys, love creates. Fear brings anxiety, and that anxiety might get so bad that they begin to ask: 'Does God really love me? Am I really saved?'"

"I've asked those same questions myself in the past," I acknowledged, "and let me tell you…it's not a good feeling being so uncertain…the feeling of hopelessness it brings."

"Precisely my point Rob," Jesus said. "This is one of the main reasons Christians leave the fold these days. I want my followers to feel the love, and not live in fear. But at the same time, as your pastor pointed out, I don't want my followers to become complacent and forget to Whom they owe everything. And I don't want them to give others the idea that my followers do not respect and revere the Lord God Almighty, so it's important to maintain a sense of holiness and sacredness when you come before me and my Father. But don't fall back on the old picture of a king sitting on a huge throne with his back to the wall and all the subjects lying flat on their faces before him... No, that would be a mistake. Do you know why the kings of old sat on big thrones with their backs to the wall? Because it was awfully hard for an enemy to sneak up and attack them when they had their backs to the wall, that's why! And why did they insist that their subjects approach them prostrate on the ground? Because it difficult for an enemy to attack you from such a position, isn't it?"

I had to admit, this last point did make me think differently about my dilemma. I saw Jesus reach over to the Bible on the table and open it up.

"My friend John put it so well I'd like to read you what he said." He opened the book and began to read. "'And so we know and rely on the love God has for us. God is love. Whoever lives in love lives in God, and God in them. This is how love is made complete among us so that we will have confidence on the Day of Judgment: in this world we are like Jesus. There is no fear in love. But perfect love drives out fear, because fear has to do with punishment. The one who fears is not made perfect in love. We love because He first loved us.'" (1 John 4:16-19)

That last verse almost made me cry. It was so true. Despite all our sins and weaknesses, God still loved us...and He has loved us from the beginning. It doesn't matter how we might "feel" about it; sometimes even a believer feels remote and lost. But God loves us in any case, even if we don't realize or remember it. And when we love Him back, with all our hearts...it drives away our fears.

"So I can still think of you as a good friend, as a 'buddy,' and we can still have these little chats on the porch?"

Jesus smiled. "Sure! As long as you…you know…remember who I am and what I did for you." Then he had a thought. "You've read the 'Narnia' books by C. S. Lewis, haven't you?"

"Yes," I answered. "And my wife and I enjoyed the movie they made few years ago too."

"Well, there ya go," he said. "Think of me just like Aslan the Lion in the story. He's nice and amicable…even soft and cuddly…but it's a mistake to think of him as 'tame.' So it's sort of like that: I am a man, but I am also your Savior…my Father and I are one with the Holy Spirit."

And suddenly Jesus' face…changed. Actually his whole body changed, but I noticed his face first. It began to glow…as if an inner light were coming from him. And his face became beautiful; not that his face wasn't beautiful before, but it had been merely a normal beautiful, not…so <u>beautiful</u>. It was actually hard to look at; I had to look away. But before I did I saw his clothing take on a radiance like a million halogen headlight shining at once. It blinded me. I looked away.

I was suddenly overcome with the same feeling Jesus had described: a deep, gut-wrenching, draining feeling that left me hollow and empty. This void inside me screamed to be filled. I felt the strong need to do…something. Anything. I just needed to do something constructive…something useful and productive. Then I thought I heard a voice, soft but quite audible, saying: "This is My Son, whom I have chosen, whom I love; listen to Him." (Luke 9:35)

Seized with awe—and there was no mistaking the feeling—I found myself kneeling before Jesus on the wooden deck of the porch. So much for that being unnatural. The next second I saw all my sins, all the bad things I was ashamed of in my life appear before me, right there in my line of vision. But I was not simply seeing them with my eyes…I was <u>feeling</u> them…experiencing them, all over again…and it hurt. It physically hurt. I couldn't breathe. I felt a weight on my chest, and for a moment I suspected a heart attack (I <u>am</u> in the prime age group after all)…but then it subsided…lifted in fact, as if a heavy load had been taken from me. I couldn't believe the gratitude I felt. I looked up, and Jesus had returned to "normal." There were copious tears in my eyes, which I had no desire to wipe away.

I had just experienced something very similar to what the apostles must have experienced on the mountain when Jesus "transfigured" himself before them. It was a way of showing them His Heavenly Glory so they would have a better understanding of who He was. Since they had only known Jesus as a human, this "transfiguration" had made quite an impression on the ones who witnessed it: Peter, James and John. But they had had a hard time comprehending what they experienced. They had wanted to erect "booths" (or tabernacles) for Jesus, and also for Elijah and Moses, who had also appeared during the transfiguration. I could understand their wanting to build some kind of tabernacle: I had experienced an urge to do something…anything…as well. And as a Christian, I knew what my Lord wanted me to do, and it was not, necessarily, to build tabernacles. It was spelled out for us in Matthew 28:19-20: "Therefore go and make disciples of all nations, baptizing them in the name of the Father and of the Son and of the Holy Spirit, and teaching them to obey everything I have commanded you." He wanted us to go and spread the Good News of Jesus Christ to the world. Now <u>that</u> is something productive that I can certainly do.

I looked up and Jesus was smiling again, that wonderful smile of his, as he gently rocked in the chair. "So you see…it's a mistake to forget Who I really am…my <u>friend!</u>" Then he winked at me.

I stood up from my kneeling position, a bit unsteadily, and sat back down in my chair. "I honestly don't see that ever slipping my mind again, Jesus."

Chapter Three: The Angry Man

My house was on a street adjacent to a busy section of town, so I saw a lot of people come and go as they passed the front of my house, both on foot and in their cars. Most of the locals I knew on sight, if not by name. Many of them living in my local neighborhood preferred to walk into downtown, where there are various stores and shops, rather than drive their cars, if the weather was good. One friend of mine who lived a few houses down was just such a resident. And he was consistent, always walking by around 10:00 am every Tuesday and Thursday, and at various times during the weekends. I remember a few months ago when I hadn't seen him for a while, I almost called the police to report a missing person. Turned out he took some time off to visit his sister in Florida.

Robert, or Bob as he liked to be called—Bob the Hat in fact, no last name that I was aware of—was an active member of the local Alcoholics Anonymous, and a bit of an infamous character at that. I'm not sure about his former life, but he had the look of a truck driver or a sailor or some other colorful character. He always wore a dirty black derby, hence the nickname that stuck even when he was away from AA. He was a gruff, angry (in an unfocused way) middle-aged guy with permanent five o'clock shadow and a few mysterious scars on his face. He usually wore loose-fitting tank-tops that displayed the colorful tattoos on his arms and shoulders. He smoked about two packs of non-filtered cigarettes a day, so he was a regular at the convenience store up on the corner.

I was sitting with Jesus on the porch when we saw Bob coming down the street. He wasn't smiling. I don't think he smiled very much. His head was bent down and he seemed to be mumbling or grumbling, almost arguing with himself. This was not unusual. Bob's fights with the devil and angel on his shoulders were often public display.

"Yo Bob!" I called as he passed the porch. I waved at him, but he didn't seem to notice. I stood up and went to the railing, waved and called to him again. "Yo! Bob! Who ya talkin' to?"

He finally lifted his head and noticed me on the porch. "Oh, hey Bob, how's it going?" He was one of the few people I allowed to call me "Bob." You just didn't correct Bob the Hat. I guess he couldn't imagine anyone named Robert being called anything but Bob. "Just arguin' with myself is all," he said.

"Arguin' about what?" I asked as he leaned up against the railing of the porch.

"Lousy [BLEEPERS] and [BLEEPERS], they should all eat [BLEEP] and [BLEEPING] die! Pardon my French." Bob's language always needed careful editing. One did it automatically, so you hardly heard the cursing.

"That wasn't French." Jesus pointed out.

"Why don't you come up to the porch and visit a while?" I asked Bob.

"Nah," he waved off the invitation. "Gotta get cigs for me and the ol' lady, and then I gotta get down to the hall and sweep up because those [BLEEPERS] don't [BLEEPING] cleanup after their [BLEEPING] selves."

I don't think Bob had a job other than taking care of the Legion Hall where AA met four times a week. "So how's the wife and kids these days?" I knew he had two children from a previous marriage. I only met his "significant other" once in the deli, and I was not sure if they were legally married, although he calls her his wife and she calls him her husband, so I guess that's common law, right?

"Don't [BLEEPING] ask, [LORD'S NAME IN VAIN] it! [BLEEPING] boy is in and out of juvie all the time, and that [BLEEPING] daughter of mine is worse than her [LORD'S NAME IN VAIN] [DEROGATORY BOVINE TERM] of a mother!"

I looked over to see how Jesus was handling all this colorful language, but he was listening calmly, taking it all in, not affected in any way I could see. He saw me look over and nodded, but didn't say anything.

I wasn't sure how to respond to Bob, and it appeared he was in a bit of a hurry, so I decided just to wish him a good day and he walked off to buy cigarettes, muttering to himself.

"Now that's a very angry man," Jesus said as Bob walked off.

"He has a lot of issues," I agreed.

"Will he be coming back this way?"

"Yeah. As soon as he stocks up on cigarettes he'll probably head right home and pass us again."

"Let's see if he'll talk to us again when he comes by," Jesus said. Then he added, "Let's not talk about him until he comes back. You know how I hate gossip."

So we settled back in our chairs, waiting and rocking; Jesus had his head bowed in his usual revere and I just watched the clouds float by. The air was still and the street relatively quiet except for the rustle of the trees and the merry chirping of the birds.

Bob came back soon enough, and I waved him over to the porch again.

"[LORD'S NAME IN VAIN] cigarettes have gone up in price again!" Bob commented as he came over to the railing.

"Yeah, I heard they were putting another tax on them, to balance the budget," I said. "Feel like setting a spell?" I enjoyed using folksy expressions like that sometimes.

"Nah, gotta get back to the ol' lady and keep her [BLEEPING] entertained or she'll run off on me!"

Jesus leaned forward. "Ask him why he's so angry?" he whispered.

"Jesus wants to know why you're so angry?" I asked him. A while back I had told Bob about my idea of talking to Jesus on my porch. I had shown him the special rocker I had bought and explained how I talked to him on my porch nearly every morning. Aside from thinking I was a bit crazy…I think he liked the idea.

"Oh he does, does he?" Bob winked. "And what makes Jesus think I'm [BLEEPING] angry?"

I laughed. "Well, you sure don't sound like a happy fellow."

"What?" Bob asked, "You'd rather I'd be whistling 'Zippy-[BLEEPING] Do Da'?"

"Couldn't hurt," I said.

"Yeah right," he turned and spat on the curb about four feet from him. "So what's the [BLEEPING] problem? Can't Jesus take a few cuss words? I thought he used to hang out with those [BLEEPERS] and tax guys and all them low-life [BLEEPERS] of society? So? He ain't heard them [BLEEPING] words before?"

Jesus leaned over to me. "He's right, you know. I used to spend time with the lowest of the low, and the language from some of them back then could have curdled milk. Worse even.

Of course," he smiled, "nobody paid much attention to them, just as they don't pay much attention to them today."

"Good point," I said.

"What point," Bob asked? I keep forgetting he can only follow my half of the conversation.

"That nobody pays much attention to you when you talk like that."

"Like what?" Bob asked.

"Like freakin' and frackin' like you do," I pointed out. "You use curse words like punctuation. In fact, to you, the 'F-word' is both a noun <u>and</u> a verb…and an adjective too! I used to talk like that when I worked in the factory, until my wife pointed out that I was starting to talk like a truck driver (and not any trucker drivers <u>she</u> knew!), and she didn't like it. I had to pay more attention to what I was saying. But if you consciously keep track of it, you can clean up your language."

"And why should I [BLEEPING] want to do that?" Bob asked.

I looked to Jesus. He shrugged. "[BLEEP] if I know," he said. Only he didn't say "bleep."

I was stunned. I didn't know what to say. Bob could see the look on my face.

"What'd he say?"

I told him. Bob bent over laughing. I looked back at Jesus, who just sat in his chair looking back at me.

"What?" he finally asked after a prolonged quizzical look on my face. "You're surprised I used that word?"

"Surprised is not even the start of it," I said.

Bob was still laughing. When he finally caught his breath he said, "Jesus wouldn't talk like that."

"Why not?" Jesus asked.

I repeated the question for Bob's benefit. "Because," Bob said patiently, "he's better than that."

"Better than what?" Jesus asked.

"Better than us!" Bob said, exasperated.

Jesus sat there thinking for a moment, and then he laughed. "You and Bob are both surprised to hear me say something like that because you attach a way of being to a simple word instead of the true character of someone." He laughed again (I loved to hear him laugh). "Well, at least I know you're listening now! I'm surprised you don't remember,

Rob. It's in my teachings. It's not the word itself; it's the feeling behind the words. Remember what I said about killing, and adultery?"

I knew what he was referring to: the time in the Gospel of Matthew, chapter five, when he was explaining to the people about some of the commandments.

"If you remember," Jesus reminded me, "What I said was: Sure there's a commandment that says 'Thou shalt not murder.' But we need to go past that to the root of the commandment, to the basis of what God wants from us, and see our anger for what it really is. I told them anyone who even says 'raca' to his brother is guilty of murder. And sure, I said the word 'raca.' That was a very nasty thing to say to a person back then you know. It literally meant 'empty-headed' or 'brainless' but really meant something like 'you worthless piece of trash' or something like that. But I wasn't talking about the word; I was talking about the feeling behind the word. I said the same thing about adultery, remember? I said all you have to do is think about committing it, and you've committed it. I stretched their limits, Rob. I told them we had to do more than just control our actions; we had to control our minds and hearts as well. It's not enough to merely <u>not</u> do something. You have to <u>want</u> to <u>not</u> do it, or it doesn't count."

I repeated what Jesus said to Bob as best I could. "So what's all that mean?" Bob asked.

"What it means, Bob, is that what goes on in your head is what comes out of your mouth, and <u>that's</u> what's bad or good. Not the words themselves, but the feelings. So either you, Bob, are angry all the time—for the words coming out of your mouth are angry words—or your words are meaningless at best and offensive at worst."

I paraphrased again for Bob. He had no response.

"I still want to know why he's so angry," Jesus said.

So I asked. "So what <u>are</u> you so mad about, Bob?"

Bob screwed his face up, giving me the look of someone who swallowed a lemon. "What d' ya mean 'What am I so mad about?' What do you think? If it's not the ol' lady going [BLEEPING] off about something of another, it's the [DARN] kids carryin' on or getting' arrested… Then there're the people down at the clinic, who won't give me any more antibiotics when I'm sick, and the [BLEEPING] phone company...not to mention the cable and electric bills, and now she wants to go down to [BLEEPING] Florida again when we [BLEEPING] just got back..."

"Whoa, Bob," I interrupted, sorry I asked. "That's a lot of stuff to be mad about."

"You tellin' me?" he chortled.

"Why don't you come up here and sit for a few minutes and we'll talk about some of it? I don't think I could tackle all of it in one sitting."

He looked up suspiciously. "You're not gonna go all religious on me with this 'talkin' to Jesus' [BOVINE EXCREMENT], are you Rob?"

"No...no, I wouldn't do that," I said, barely able to hide my excitement at hearing him call me "Rob" for a change. "But sit over here," I indicated an old stool he could sit on. "That rocker is still for Jesus you know." I winked, and he nodded, but still didn't smile.

"Like I said," he added cautiously once he settled into the stool. "Don't you go gettin' all holy rollin' on me or anything."

"Nah, Bob, I'll just let you know what Jesus says, no big deal."

"Well...okay then."

Jesus sat there for a moment studying Bob. "You know," he said after a while, "there is such a thing as righteous anger. There are some things worth getting angry about. We were just talking the other day about worrying, weren't we? There are some things it's necessary to worry over; just as there are some things it's important to be angry about. It's okay to become angry over the evils of the world, injustice, cruelty and things intolerable to decent people. But the opportunity—and yes it's an opportunity—to be angry over these types of truly evil situations are fewer in most people's lives than you think. What's more common, I'm afraid, is the anger that leads nowhere: that's unproductive, that hurts people in many different ways. The anger that simmers—boils and scalds the soul—and kills. This type of anger is often a primary cause of sin."

I was rehashing all this for Bob as Jesus went along. "Wait a minute," Bob said. "There're lots of things that make a person angry these days, man! You can't just shrug them off."

"Nothing <u>makes</u> you angry except yourself," Jesus said. "You're the only influence that really counts; no one can 'make' you be anything. Only <u>you</u> can make yourself be as you want to be. That's your God-given 'free will.'"

"Oh! Here we go!" Bob exploded. "The ol' 'free will' [BLEEP]! Why does it always come down to that?"

"Because," Jesus said, "that's all you really have."

"Huh?" Bob said.

"That's all you got, buddy!" Jesus answered again. "The only thing that's truly yours. What? You think you own your house, or your car? You can't take it with you, right? How about your soul? Yeah, that's right? Is that really yours? Nope! That belongs to my Father. So what do you really have? Free will, that's what you have!"

I had never seen Jesus expound in this way, and it puzzled me. "And your point is?" I asked, trying to make some simple sense out of his reference to free will.

He smiled, leaned back against the rocker and said: "Why don't you try a little experiment?"

"Me, or Bob?"

"Both of you. Try this: The next time you get angry, exercise your free will. You, and only you, decide how to act and behave and <u>feel</u> from one moment to the next. So use your free will, and go <u>against</u> what you believe you're really feeling. Do the exact opposite of what you would do normally, or at least what you consider normal for yourself."

"I'm not sure I follow," I said. "You mean, if I feel angry, I should…laugh?"

"Exactly!" Jesus said.

"That's [BLEEPING] nuts!" said Bob, adding his opinion.

"What's nuts about it?" Jesus asked. "You know you have the power to do it, you just never use the power. Oh, you do sometimes, if you're in an embarrassing situation or for some overwhelming reason you <u>must</u> act contrary to your anger…maybe in those situations you use your power over yourself to 'put on a happy face' or 'keep a stiff upper lip' or whatever you call it."

"Well yeah," I said, "those are times when it's necessary to put on a mask, or use the <u>power</u> as you say."

"And who decides what's necessary? You do. So decide. Decide it's necessary the next time you get angry; decide it's necessary to act completely different. Laugh, as you suggested, instead of shouting out in anger. Force your scowl into a smile, and make yourself think of more pleasant things. Purposely <u>change your mind</u> and take a different path. That's what 'repent' really means you know: to change one's mind. So just once, use it to prove something to yourself."

"Prove what?" I asked.

"Prove that you have my Father's gift of free will and can change any unpleasant situation for the better simply by using it. And think of me. Through me you can do anything, anywhere, anytime.

"Philippians, chapter four, verse thirteen," I quoted: "'I can do all things in Christ, Who strengthens me.'"

"Right!" Jesus said.

I explained to Bob what Jesus had proposed. "So let me get this straight," he said. "The next time I get angry...which won't be too [BLEEPING] long, that's for sure...I'm supposed to act the [BLEEPING] exact opposite I would normally [BLEEPING] act?"

"Yup," I said, "without the frackin' and stuff."

Bob sat on the stool and thought about that for a few seconds. "I don't know," he said, rubbing the stubble on his chin. "Sounds [BLEEPING] nuts to me...but okay, I'll give it a [BLEEPING] try, just for you ol' buddy!" He winked, got up, and went on his way.

"'Don't let the sun go down while you are still angry,'" Jesus called after him. Paul's words in Ephesians 4:26.

"There's a reason Paul said that," Jesus said to me as we watched Bob walk away. "When you hold on to your anger it ferments inside you and can lead in all sorts of nasty directions. Best to do away with angry feelings right away, before they get too strong."

"You mentioned 'righteous anger.'" I wanted to hear more on what he meant by that.

"Yes, there's that." He leaned forward so our heads were closer. "The kind of anger that provokes actions for the good, not just for selfish revenge or pointless retribution."

"But how can you tell which anger you're feeling?"

"Well, use your mind and sort it out," he said. "A lot of selfish anger comes from fear. Actually a lot of negativity has its basis in fear. It's one of the 'mother' emotions: it gives rise to other feelings like anger and worry and sadness."

"So if you can tell your anger is based on fear, that's the wrong kind of anger?"

Jesus nodded warily. "Sort of like that, but not exactly." He stood up and started to pace around the porch. "Here's an example. Say you're walking down the street, and you see a large man abusing a small child. He's hitting the child with his fists right there on the street. Now, for most people, this will provoke an angry response. What they're witnessing is <u>wrong</u>. They know it to their inner-most being. It is <u>wrong</u>. And it's righteous anger that usually causes them to interfere on the child's behalf. That's an example of anger used in the right way." He sat down and looked at me for a response.

I thought for a moment. "But is it really <u>that</u> simple?"

"Sure it is," Jesus said. "And that example is not as simple as I made it sound. In most people there's an equal and opposite <u>fear</u> emotion, the: 'I don't want to get involved' syndrome. Most people, especially in areas with high populations like inner cities, are afraid to get involved in potentially dangerous situations. Remember, I said a <u>large</u> man. He could just a soon turn around and start pounding on <u>you</u>. Or worse! These thoughts inevitably go through everyone's mind in this sort of situation. But most of us in this situation would overcome our fear; righteous anger would trump the selfish fear response and most of us would try to stop the man from further abusing the child, regardless of the possible consequences to ourselves. Do you see what I mean?"

"Sure," I said, "in <u>that</u> situation I see what you mean. But most situations in life are not that simple. How do you know when your anger is 'righteous'?"

"What do you mean?" Jesus asked.

"Well, like when you get angry at some idiot cutting you off in traffic?"

"Some idiot?" he repeated. "You mean a 'raca'?"

"Okay, bad example," I corrected. "How about when they rip you off at the store…"

"Rip you off? You mean rob you?"

"No, I mean when they charge those high prices and use those phony gimmicks."

"Sounds like business as usual to me Rob," Jesus said.

"How about when some moron steps in front of you in line at the grocery store?"

"Raca," Jesus said again.

"The trash bag rips open and spills all the garbage on the kitchen floor…"

"Poor me," he said. "The evil trash bag has conspired with the kitchen floor to ruin my day."

"The gas man is hours late from the time the gas company said he'd be there…"

"My time is just soooo valuable," Jesus said.

"Okay, hang on…" I was trying to come up with a good example. Then I thought I had one. "Okay, how about when your neighbor borrows your hedge-clippers and never returns them as he promised…."

"Give him your lawn mower too," Jesus said simply, looking right into my eyes.

He could be sly sometimes. He was making another reference to the Sermon on the Mount, in Matthew chapter five, verse 40, where Jesus said: "If anyone wants to sue you and take your shirt, let him have your coat also." He said this right after the "turn the other cheek" passage. He was telling me, in his own inscrutable way, that most of what I think is real anger is actually selfish anger. Most of what gets me angry (and Jesus would remind me that only I can get myself angry, other things don't get me angry) are essentially trivial and egocentric. But real anger—true anger—the kind that leads to justice and fairness, that's anger as humans are supposed to experience it.

"It's the same with fear," Jesus said. "Say you're in a field one spring day, and a thunder storm is approaching. The lightning and thunder cause fear to rise up in you like a hot-air balloon in your belly. So you run for shelter, afraid for your life. Now, <u>that's</u> a good kind of fear: it caused you to take steps to protect yourself, and that's a good thing, right? But at the same time that same fear of thunder and an approaching storm can become irrational. Suppose you're sufficiently protected and out of danger, but you are paralyzed with fear nonetheless. That's the wrong kind of fear, because everything that could be done has been done and you are safe."

I nodded. "Yes, I follow you."

"Sometimes my Father and I can't help wondering," Jesus continued, "when we see so many people living in fear all the time. And perpetual fear can cause perpetual anger, sadness, loss of joy…all of that. We wonder why they feel that way. Don't they understand that my Father has their best interests at heart? Don't they know how much I love them? I guess not, because if they did, they wouldn't feel so afraid all the time. The prophet Isaiah said, 'I am surrounded by trouble, but You protect me against my angry enemies with Your powerful arm, You keep me safe (Isaiah 138:7).' The prophet seemed to understand that with God you need not fear. That's why David said in his psalm, 'I will fear no evil, for You are with me; Your rod and your staff, they comfort me (Psalm 23:4).' If more people knew this, maybe they wouldn't be so selfish and afraid all the time; and then maybe there wouldn't be as much self-centered anger in the world."

"Amen," I said to that.

Chapter Four: The Grieving Mother

It was a Tuesday, and my unemployment check had been deposited, so I decided to go to the grocery store for some much-needed supplies. By chance I met one of my neighbors, Mrs. Hummel, in the frozen food section.

"Good Morning Mrs. Hummel, how are you today," I said when I saw her.

She looked up from the package of frozen peas she was scrutinizing. "Oh, hello Rob. I'm all right," was her insincere reply. "How are you?"

"I'm fine Mrs. Hummel," I answered. I noticed the drawn look on her face. "Is something bothering you?"

She bowed her head and said softly, "I'm just having some trouble coping with the loss of my daughter."

Her youngest daughter had died of cancer last month. It was a terrible shock to the family, especially to Mrs. Hummel, since she had only just lost her husband a few years ago. She was a nice, middle-aged Christian woman who'd never hurt a fly, and she was always friendly, at least to me. I hated to see her so distraught. I thought I should say something comforting, but I couldn't think of anything to say. And this concerned me. So I brought the subject up with Jesus the next morning.

"Good mornin' Jesus."

"Good mornin' Rob. How are you doing today?"

"Well, I'm fine, but something has me concerned."

Jesus leaned over in his chair. "And what might that be," he asked.

"I was talking to Mrs. Hummel yesterday, I think I might have mentioned her to you...the woman whose daughter died of cancer last month?"

"Yes, I remember you mentioning her," Jesus said.

"She and I were talking in the grocery store yesterday, and she seemed so down and depressed. She's not handling the loss of her daughter very well, and...well, I thought I should be able to comfort her with some kind words or something like that. But I couldn't think of anything to say that would make any difference to her."

Jesus sat there for a moment, then he nodded. "I understand. Losing a child is the worst thing that can happen to anyone. And it's never easy to get over it. In the old days it was common for children to die young; two out of three babies never made it through their first year, and the odds didn't improve much as they got older. But it was never easy to cope with the loss. It's like having your heart torn out. Not a wound that heals easily."

"But her daughter was so young," I said sadly. "I met her once. She was young and full of life. Now she's dead. It's just not right. It wasn't fair that her youngest daughter should be taken away from her."

Jesus sighed. "Do I need to remind you there's no guarantee for life to be fair? Don't you know that my Father in Heaven weeps at the falling of a sparrow, so how much more does He weep for one dying so young? Or do you think my Father caused the death of the young woman?"

I was humbled by his words. A lot of people blamed God for bad things happening, for the death of infants, for tragic losses and the sometimes horrible suffering of the innocent. Many blamed God, but their blame was misdirected. God does not <u>make</u> bad things happen to good people, just as He doesn't cause good things to happen to bad people. God doesn't interfere with the natural progression of the world. When God interacts with the world He mostly does so <u>through us</u>.

"No," I answered, "I know God is not to blame for her death. But it's so hard to talk to people when tragedy hits, so difficult to find the right words, to say the things that will make a difference."

"Just say what's in your heart."

"And what does that mean?" I asked heatedly. "What do you mean, 'Say what's in your heart.' If I could do that, I wouldn't be asking you what to say, would I?" My frustration was palatable, but I shouldn't have taken it out on Jesus. I could see he was hurt by my words. I really should think before I say things. But he didn't respond with a comeback; he didn't attack me with words. He just sat quietly, looking at me.

"I'm sorry," I offered. "I didn't mean to snap at you like that. It's just that you make it sound so easy, to say what's in my heart. But it's not easy; I can't find the right words."

"Rob, sometimes there are no 'right words' to say."

"But you always seem to say the right things!"

Jesus was silent once again. He just looked at me with those brown eyes. I knew he wanted me to say something more, but to be honest I had no idea what he was expecting from me.

Jesus finally spoke. "You seem to be waiting for me to say something."

"Well, yeah...I am."

"And what would you have me say?" he asked.

This threw me. Obviously my Christian education and upbringing should be giving me words to say for just such a situation. But my brain was failing me. I tried thinking of all those wise folk in the Bible and what they would have said. I tried thinking about how I had heard pastors and other ministers comfort the grieving, even for such a loss as this. But I was coming up blank.

"I'm coming up blank Jesus," I said finally.

Jesus nodded. "You know, there's really nothing anyone can say that will truly take the pain away from one who is grieving. The loss is real, and the loved one can never be replaced, and will never be forgotten. Tell me," he asked, "what would you like to hear if you suffered such a loss?"

"Me?"

"Yeah, you."

"Hmm. Well, I guess I would like to hear something about Heaven; that my loved one was with God and in a better place. Maybe something about birth and death being part of life..."

"Kind of cliché and a little corny, don't you think?" commented Jesus.

"Then what would <u>you</u> say to her?" I asked.

"I can tell you what Paul said," he answered, and reached for the Bible I kept on a table on the porch. "Here, in his first letter to the Thessalonians, chapter four, verse 14, he wrote: 'We believe that Jesus died and rose again and so we believe that God will bring with Jesus those who have fallen asleep in him.' And in Second Corinthians, chapter one, verse nine, he writes: 'Indeed, in our hearts we felt the sentence of death. But this happened that we might not rely on ourselves but on God, who raises the dead.'"

I allowed that to sink in. "That's all well and good for what Paul has to say about death, but what would <u>you</u> say to Mrs. Hummel?" I was very curious to hear what Jesus would say to her.

He thought for a moment. "I wouldn't say very much. A lot of times it's all just words, and that's all the person hears, just the words. When I was told of Lazarus's death I was inconsolable. I was telling myself the same platitudes you mentioned. But I knew that wasn't enough, not for the people around me at the time. So I demonstrated that no one who believes in me is ever really dead."

The story of how Jesus raised Lazarus from the dead is told in the Gospel of John. It's a powerful, touching story, but I was taking away a completely different meaning from what Jesus meant. And, I'll admit it, I was becoming a little frustrated.

"But you raised Lazarus, your friend, from the dead. I can't do anything like that for Mrs. Hummel. And I can't, or wouldn't, ask you to do something like that for her either. So where does that leave me?"

We were sitting facing each other. Jesus stood up from his chair and put his arms on my shoulders and smiled. "'I tell you for certain that everyone who hears my message and has faith in the one who sent me has eternal life and will never be condemned. They have already gone from death to life.'" (John 5:24)

My eyes filled with tears, as they often do when Jesus hits me with a potent truth.

He sat down. "One truth I can definitely tell anyone who suffers a terrible loss is that I share their sorrow. My Father feels the same pain for the loss, although they may not believe that at the time. No one loses anyone alone. I am with them; I grieve with them and weep with them. My love for them enfolds them. The compassion I share with them for any horrible loss is the most real thing in the universe, and will never go away. What can I do? Should I open my heart to these people? I already have. All they have to do is take it. I am with them in the best and worst moments of their lives, always."

I was listening closely, but I still wasn't sure there was anything I could say to Mrs. Hummel that might bring her some comfort. I think Jesus sensed this.

"Think about this," he suggested. "My Father suffered the loss of a child, His only son, and willingly because He loved all of you here on the earth so much. But He still felt the loss, just as you do, more so in fact than you can ever imagine. My Father and I also feel the same pain as you do for the losses you must ultimately suffer in this life. This goes for each and every one of you. So it's a blessing to be able to share this emotion with God, knowing He feels the loss as much or more than you. Sure you'll cry; you'll cry a lot, but the Lord weeps with you. Yes, you'll hurt, but as the song goes: 'everybody hurts.' That's why God gave you each other. And there's the sunshine, and all the simple blessings my Father bestows on you all the time, to lighten your heart. The Lord will not abandon you, even in your darkest times."

I was trying to understand everything he said, and let his words sink in. It's true, I thought; after all, God had to witness His only son being nailed to a cross. He had to watch as His only son suffered and died at the hands of humans. And then I thought of Mary, Jesus' mother. She too had to watch as her son died on the cross. So much suffering. But God tells us in the Bible that this is not the end, not the final act of the grand play we call 'Life.' We know Jesus rose from the dead, and that we will follow him some day, we don't know when. But a glorious finish awaits us, as we are promised, after we move on from this life. In the end we'll be with the Lord and His son. There will be no more suffering.

I looked up at Jesus, his beautiful face, his dark, knowing eyes. He was smiling slightly, and I smiled back. "I guess I should try to tell Mrs. Hummel something like that," I suggested. "But coming from me, I'm not sure it would bring much comfort to her."

He sat down with a flop, and the chair wobbled in protest. "Most people in mourning don't want words of comfort. They don't really want you to take their suffering away. There's a reason for suffering, and most people when they're going through it recognize the vital quality of it; it's cathartic, it helps them deal with the loss, with the tragedy. It feels appropriate.

Taking that away from them would be a disservice. All they really want or need from you or anyone is to share in their grief, to understand their sorrow, and to show them they're not alone, that others feel the loss too."

The next day I walked over to Mrs. Hummel's house, a couple of blocks from mine. She welcomed me and we sat and talked a while, sipping coffee and making nice chit-chat. Then I asked her about her daughter, and she began to cry. I told her what Jesus had told me, and she nodded, still crying. I held her hand and told her I wanted her to know that I felt her sorrow at the loss, how unfair it seemed and how horrible it was to have to live with the loss. And then I told her again what Jesus said. I quoted the verse from John. I think she understood. When I left I felt much better. You know… I think that whole episode was mostly for my benefit, and only a little for Mrs. Hummel.

INTERLUDE

I woke this morning in a particularly foul mood, which happens from time to time. I usually attribute it to a bad dream or indigestion from dinner the previous night, but I know there's really no reason for it. I'm just in a lousy mood this morning. No big deal.

I got my cup of coffee and went out to the porch. Jesus was there, as usual, siting in the rocker, his head bowed and his hands to his lips. He wasn't praying; when he prayed he knelt, bowed his head, folded his hands and placed them on his forehead. No, this was his reflective posture: he was merely being in the moment, appreciating his Father's creation.

"'Mornin' Jesus," I said as I sat down, leaving off the "good" as I didn't want to be hypocritical in my morning greeting.

"'Mornin' Rob," he echoed back to me with a slight nod. Then he closed his eyes again and resumed his revere.

It was a typical weekday morning, with people coming and going and cars buzzing by; I could hear the hum of cars on the highway not too far from my house. One of my neighbors had their television turned up way too high; I could hear it clearly from half a block away. I recognized the game show. A car drove by with windows down and radio blasting, rap music bombarding the neighborhood. I didn't see much to appreciate of God's creation, and I said so.

There are mornings when Jesus isn't in a talkative mood. This was one of those mornings. He just opened his eyes and raised his eyebrows in that way he does, acknowledging my opinion but silently disagreeing with me just the same. A smile came to his lips but he didn't speak. He closed his eyes again and took a deep breath. The smile remained.

I suddenly felt defensive. "What? You mean you can find something to appreciate this morning in all this chaos?" He just looked at me, still smiling. "Oh, okay, let me see… There's the sunshine, right? We can appreciate the God-given sunshine on our face, is that it? Well, that same sunshine can cause cancer you know, and you can die from too much sunshine, so what's to appreciate in that?"

He sat back, no longer smiling, but listening, eyes open, attentive, but still silent.

"Oh, the wind in our face? The gentle breeze? Right! That same 'gentle breeze' can turn into a hurricane or tornado and wipe out your home."

He just sat and listened. My defensiveness was losing energy. I knew what he wanted me to say. Isn't that always the way it is? It seems you argue with God all your life, and all the while, you <u>know</u> what He wants you to do. You know it in your heart. So in a sense, you're really arguing with yourself.

I sat back, all the fight taken out of me. I couldn't seem to remember what I was so worked up about. I took a sip of coffee. It sure was good this morning. I'll have to tell my wife she made a great pot of coffee today. It was just the way I liked it: not too light, not too sweet, and no burnt coffee taste, just that rich mocha flavor. I let the sip trickle down slowly, savoring the taste. Ah. Now that's something you can appreciate: God's gift of coffee. Or, for that matter, God's gift of taste buds so we can appreciate the taste of coffee. And don't forget the smell. Ah, the smell is almost better than the taste! What a wonderful thing it is to be able to appreciate a cup of coffee in the morning. And I'm unemployed; I don't deserve it. But I have it every morning just the same. Just as we say, "Give us this day our daily bread" in the Lord's Prayer, but we get our daily bread every day anyway, whether we ask for it or not, whether we deserve it or not. It's the same with God's grace. I don't deserve it (no way!), but I get it, every day. Now <u>that's</u> something to appreciate.

I looked up and saw Jesus watching me. He winked.

"I know:" I said to his unspoken question, "perspective." I winked back at him. A bird flew by, a purple martin, soaring into the air in front of the porch and doing acrobatics for us. I was aware that even the hum of the cars on the highway seemed to lend a gentle background drone to the day. It was late July and I could hear the early cicadas' high-pitched buzzing in the trees in the distance. Their buzzing seemed to go in concert with the highway hum, and that, coupled with the constant chirping of the birds, gave the morning its soundtrack: a funky, rhythmic drone, as a whispering murmur in the air. It gave the morning color. It seemed to set the pace for everybody going about their business as I watched from my porch.

"So you see it now?" Jesus asked. By "see" he meant much more than just seeing with my eyes, and by "it" he meant all of God's blessings that stretched out before us every day.

"Yes, I see it now." I wanted to apologize to him. "Sorry about the grumpy start. I just get up on the wrong side of bed sometimes."

"And which side is that?"

"It's just an expression," I said, smiling. He often did that when I used a colloquialism.

"I never get tired of just sitting here being in my Father's creation," he said. "I want everyone to be able to do it, all the time."

"I know," I said, "but sometimes it's just hard to see it for what it really is. We're just humans, and things get to us sometimes, and we're not always in a good mood."

"Yes…I know. It's not easy being you."

He was repeating my own words back to me, another trick he used when I was feeling sorry for myself.

"I need to learn to appreciate just being alive I guess."

Jesus sat back in his chair. "Why not try right now?"

"Okay. Sure."

He sat up straight. "Take a deep breath…" he indicated I should inflate my lungs to capacity, "…and let it out. Good. Now relax. Keep your eyes open. Sit back. Relax…breathe. Smell the air…"

I was sitting with my back straight in the chair, my head slightly tilted, softly inhaling the air. My eyes were open so I could see the clouds gently floating by like feathers in the sky. I let my mind drift to the first time I flew in an airplane as a child. My parents let me sit in the window seat. I couldn't take my eyes off the tops of the beautiful, puffy clouds as we flew over them. They were just so…beautiful. Like soft feathery pillows. Like grandmas' feather-bed. I imagined, in my child's mind, that this is what Heaven would be like: soft, feathery…eternally safe. I sighed at the memory and the childish thought of Heaven.

"'Come to me, all you who are weary and burdened, and I will give you rest.'"

I heard Jesus' soft whisper as tears filled my eyes.

"'Take my yoke upon you and learn from me, for I am gentle and humble in heart, and you will find rest for your soul,'" he said to me. "'For my yoke is easy, and my burden is light.'" (Matthew 11:28-30)

I wiped the tears from my eyes, no embarrassment in front of my Savior. "I just forget sometimes Jesus, I forget..."

"Forget what?" he asked gently.

I wasn't really sure. "I don't know. I forget about God's love... I forget about God's gifts. I forget about what you did for us all...and what that means to me. I sometimes think I don't deserve it, so I won't get it, and that's that right of it, because I really don't deserve it, and when I get that in my mind it's very easy to see the hate and the garbage in the world, because it's all around, all the time. I just forget, is all..." I was babbling, so I stopped. I didn't know what else to say.

Jesus paused for a second or two, and then he spoke. "I know how hard it is to live everyday as if it's the last day of your life. But that's a fact, Rob: each day could be your last day. So don't waste it in a bad mood."

"Easier..."

"...said than done,'" Jesus finished for me, not even giving me time to finish one of my favorite sayings. "I know... But don't you see? When you let all those things get in the way of God's love, when you let all those things bring you down so you can't find God's grace in anything, that's when you have to remember that _nothing_ can separate you from God's love. Do you really think I won't be here for you, even when you can't see me sitting in this chair? Don't you know I love you more than you'll ever know? My good friend Paul said it best when he said: "'For I am convinced that neither death, nor life, nor angels, nor principalities, nor things present, nor things to come, nor powers, nor height, nor depth, nor any created thing, will be able to separate us from the love of God which is in Christ Jesus our Lord.'" (Romans 8:38-39)

I nodded. He was, of course, right again. There was nothing else to be said. We both just sat there, breathing in the air, watching the birds fly, listening to the hum of the world as it spun in its ever-present comings and goings. Life went on. And you know...I felt pretty good.

Chapter Five: The Agnostic

One of my good friends, a history professor at a local college, lives in the town just north of mine. Matt is a self-proclaimed agnostic, which to me is a polite atheist. He says he believes in God but that's as far as he goes. He doesn't believe in Jesus or the Christian message, or anything supernatural as he puts it. We met in college and we're still good friends, despite our differences.

I received a phone call from Matt one evening and we had a nice talk. One thing led to another and we got on the topic of religion.

"Honestly Rob, I really can't figure out how you can buy into all this Christian stuff," he said to me over the phone. "It's a fairy tale you know."

I had had this discussion before with Matt, and it was always stimulating, though unproductive from my point of view. "It's not a fairy tale, Matt. It's the truth. Why can't you believe that?"

"Well, for one, it's all been done before."

"What do you mean?" I asked.

"I mean the story of a god-man dying and coming back from the dead has been told long before Jesus came on the scene. The Isis and Osiris story from Egypt is about a god-man being murdered and then coming back to life. The tales told about Krishna in India and Horus in Egypt before the time of Christ parallel the Jesus story almost exactly."

"But those were all stories," I said defensively. "They are not true."

"Oh, and the stories from your Bible are true?"

"Well, yeah," I said.

"How so?" he asked.

"Well..." and I hesitated. I wanted to say something intelligent, something smart and witty that would make him see the light and believe in the Bible as I did. But I couldn't come up with anything, smart or otherwise, to answer his question. I could only think of one word. "Faith!" I said.

Matt laughed on the phone. "Right. Faith. Easy. For you maybe, but faith like that doesn't come easily for people like me."

"What do you mean 'like you'?" I asked.

"You know…educated people…" He paused. I guess he thought he was being insulting. "I don't mean you're not educated. I mean highly educated…no, I mean scientifically educated people…oh heck, you know what I mean."

"But Matt," I said, "I'm educated. You know that. I took the same science courses you took in college. But I believe the Bible."

"I know," he admitted, "that's why I'm so puzzled. How can a smart guy like you buy into all that propaganda and myth?"

"It's not myth Matt; it's history." I was immediately sorry I had used <u>that</u> word.

"<u>History</u>!" he quickly responded. "History you say? Don't talk to me about history. I know history, and the Bible was never meant to be history. It's religious myths with some historical markers to make it seem authentic, but it's still a pack of lies."

Now he was getting personal. "It's not a pack of lies Matt. Why do you say that?"

"Why?" he asked. "How can you ask me that? The main character of the Bible is a jealous spirit in the sky who makes demands on people and then kills them for not following his rules. The Jesus you're so enamored with probably didn't really exist, and the stories told in the New Testament have been copied from other religions such as Mithraism and other mystery cults from the Middle East, like the worship of Adonis and Dionysus, or the story of Horus that I already mentioned."

"Yeah, you mentioned that. What do you mean?"

"Okay, let's take the Horus story. Horus was said to be born on December 25th, and his mother was a virgin. Sound familiar? His birth was accompanied by a star in the east and he was adored and welcomed by three kings. At the age of twelve he was a prodigal child teacher, at the age of 30 he started to preach and do miracles with his disciples, who numbered…any guesses…<u>twelve</u>. Coincidence?"

"I didn't know any of that. Is that really true?"

"Rob, stories from the life of Horus had been circulating for centuries before Jesus' birth."

"But that doesn't mean they were copied," I replied.

"Rob," Matt said patiently, "the disciples back then were at the crossroads of the world. They were on the major path between the East and West. There were always travelers on the trade route; Jesus and the disciples lived in a hub of activity for many different cultures. The area where Jesus is said to have lived was very metropolitan. There is no way he and the disciples wouldn't have been aware of these myths and stories. They knew of them, and they copied them."

I was losing my argument with Matt, and I knew it. "What possible motive would the disciples and the authors of the Bible have for copying the myths from other cultures?"

"Authenticity my friend. They used those same stories to give a ring of truth to the yarns they were spinning. The most dominant religious cult back then was fertility cult of Dionysus, which also included a god who was nailed on a crucifix and then rose again from the dead. And the Norse god, Odin; he was also nailed to a tree and had a spear driven into him. If people recognized the story they might be more inclined to believe it. And these stories have a proven track record. They touch people. They work. So the writers of the Bible adopted those same stories."

"But Matt," I said, "do _you_ believe those stories of Odin and Dionysus and all that?"

"No, of course I don't! They're just stories. But that's my point: the Bible is not a revelation from God either. To me it's nonsensical to call anything a revelation that comes to us second-hand, either orally or in writing. No, for me…I'll put my faith—such as it is—in science."

I was flustered. "But science only has part of the story. It doesn't have all of the answers; it's limited. It doesn't take into account man's soul, or God, or Jesus."

"No, of course not. Science is only concerned with facts, provable facts. None of those things you mentioned are provable facts. So science ignores them."

"But God said…"

"There you go again," he interrupted. "God said this, and God said that…how do you know God said anything?"

"It's written in the Bible, and the Bible is the divine revelation of God," I answered.

"And there's another thing," he said, changing the subject. "How can a revelation from God, given in a specific time and place, be the benchmark for the whole world before the event happened and people after the event who know nothing of it…how can this be right? Why would God punish those who never heard of Jesus?"

I had heard this argument before, from Matt and from other non-believers as well. This was a hard argument to respond to for a Christian, mainly because I and other Christians also had a problem with this concept. It's difficult to believe a loving God would spread His forgiving message in such a haphazard way. Of course it's incredibly presumptuous to try to judge the will or motives of God. But I'm only human, and humans ask questions. I have always had reservations about the exclusiveness of Christianity.

"Hello," Matt said into the phone. "Hello? Is anybody there? Rob, you there?"

"I'm here Matt. I just can't think of anything to say."

"Hey pal, I never meant to trample your garden. I'm sorry if I've upset you."

"No, you haven't upset me." Then I thought for a moment. "Well, maybe a little. Truth is: I have some of the same issues with Christianity, with its exclusiveness. I mean, it's pretty clear: you either believe in Jesus or you burn in hell. But Matt, I can't for the life of me believe this is the way it really is. Can this really be true? Would God really do that? I really don't know!"

The phone call ended amicably enough, but there was a bug in my head that wouldn't leave, so the next morning I brought up the phone call with Matt to Jesus.

"Good morning Jesus."

"Good mornin' Rob." he replied from the rocking chair. "And how are you doing today?"

I told him about my conversation with Matt, and how it had upset and puzzled me. Then I sat back and waited to hear what he would say.

He sat with his eyes closed, thinking. After a short while he opened his eyes and smiled. "Nothing really new about those arguments, Rob. And he's partially right. The Bible was not meant to be history, not the kind of history you're talking about, and it's certainly not a science textbook. It's a handbook for life, given to us by God, through man. But why did the phone call upset you so much?"

"Why? How can you ask that? This guy was trashing the Bible and the Christian message, and I think I may have some of the same misgivings."

"Do you really?" Jesus asked.

"Well, yeah, some. What Matt was saying about those other religions and cultures, and how it seems the apostles and the authors of the New Testament borrowed stuff from those other 'mystery cults' as Matt called them."

"You mean like the Horus story?"

"Yeah, like that, and the Adonis story and the Osiris story… The same themes and even some of the details are the same as your story, Jesus."

"Really?" he asked.

He didn't seem to be taking this as seriously as I was. "Look," I said, "I trust Matt, and I know he is a very knowledgeable guy in history and all that, so I tend to take what he says as fact, unless I can prove him wrong."

"Have you tried?"

"What do you mean?" I asked.

"I mean, have you tried to prove him wrong? Or are you taking everything he says at face value? People can be wrong, or mistaken you know."

So I took him up on it and went to the library the next morning. I got online and started doing some research. But, of course, you really can't trust the information you find online, so once I had a good idea of the topics I was interested in I went to the huge reference section the library had and began pulling mammoth tomes and encyclopedias down from the shelves. In a short while I had the table I was sitting at piled high with different reference volumes. I was surprised by what I found.

I presented my research to Jesus the next morning. I had discovered that most of the alleged pagan parallels to the story of Jesus were actually late additions to the myths made after the resurrection of Jesus, that is to say, after the year 1 AD. In many cases, such as the story of Adonis, the parallels are a stretch. For example, the story goes that Adonis was killed by a wild boar, or by another jealous god who turned into a boar to kill him. This wasn't like the death of Jesus and his resurrection at all.

Same with the Mithras myth. His story has him slaying the "great bull of the Sun," and thus did Mithras sacrificing himself for the peace of the world. So okay, this god-man died while slaying a bull, to bring peace to the world. Nice, but not very similar to the Gospels.

And that wasn't all. The story of Adonis is ancient. It goes back thousands of years, and many scholars think it actually started as the cult of the Sumerian god Tammuz, which goes back as far as 3000 B.C. Tammuz was allegedly resurrected by the goddess Ishtar. I say "alleged" because the really ancient documents do not have the end of the story. The ending was appended ages later. What the story does include is that Tammuz did not return from death to an earthly life, but was placed in the underworld as a substitution for the goddess Ishtar. This story is nothing like the resurrection story of Jesus. And the story became intertwined with the Greek story of Adonis. So the stories became mixed up and changed through the ages. Eventually the myth-makers added a sort of "resurrection" part to the story, but this was a late addition. This could have been in response to the Christian story of Jesus for all anyone knows.

In my research I didn't find anything to convince me there were true parallels to the Christian Gospel. The story of Isis and Osiris is just as old as the Tammuz-Adonis myth, and just as tainted with additions and modifications as other old myths, perhaps more so. But the stories were not similar to the New Testament, not in any meaningful way for me. I found nothing like the Good News we have in Jesus. I found nothing to explain the empty tomb, the early belief of the disciples in the resurrection of Jesus, the eyewitness testimonies to the resurrection, the transformation of the disciples, the conversion of Paul, and the conversion of the other persons mentioned in the New Testament, etc., etc.

But I was not coming up with much ammunition to counter Matt's statement about the exclusiveness of Christianity. I was intimidated by John 14:6: "I am the way and the truth and the life. No one comes to the Father except through me." I was stuck.

"Sounds like you did your homework," he said when I was finished explaining my findings.

"Yes I did." I was proud of the research I had done. Then I told Jesus about my problem with Christian exclusiveness. He listened attentively, politely. "So you see," I finally said, "I have a problem. I don't know how to respond to Matt about the question of Christian exclusiveness."

"And you think this 'exclusiveness' is unique to Christianity?" he asked.

"Well, yeah, I guess," I said. "At least I never heard of any other religion having a problem with it."

"Rob, the reason it's a 'problem' for you is because you don't understand. Exclusiveness is not unique to Christianity. It's a large part of any 'religion' these days. All religions use some kind of exclusion policy of one sort or another. It's a way to define who belongs to a faith. But you know me, Rob, and you know my Father. What you don't know is how my Father will ultimately fulfill His will."

"What do you mean?"

"You've read Revelation in the Bible, right?" he asked.

"Sure. Can't say I understood much of it, but yeah, I've read it and we studied it in Bible Class at church."

"Good. It's a difficult book to understand. It's written in a type of poetry that was very popular back in my day, but Homer reads easier than this stuff. Revelation does talk about who will be in in Heaven, though. In chapter five, verse nine, it says: 'And they sang a new song: You are worthy to take the scroll and to open its seals, because you were slain, and with your blood you purchased men for God from <u>every tribe and language and people and nation</u> (emphasis mine).'"

I didn't see what Jesus was getting at. "So what does that mean?" I asked.

"Don't you see Rob? It's saying there will be people in Heaven from every country and every major culture or group in history. Not just Christians. Not just Jews, or Muslims, or Hindus…but: '…every tribe…language…people and nation.'"

I still was not following Jesus. I think he saw the puzzlement in my face.

"Well, it means that whatever goes on in the world, however the Christian message gets spread, passed from person to person and believed by the people of the world, scripturally you have to account for every tribe and language and people and nation. There will be people from all groups in Heaven."

I was stunned. Yet there it was, in Revelation, a scripture saying there will be folks from all groups on earth in Heaven; all divisions of people will be represented. Somehow the Good News will reach even the most remote people in the world. "But that is amazing, Jesus. How will God's Word reach all those groups of people?"

"That's what I was saying before," he said. "Except for your part in the plan, which is an integral part believe me, you can't know. No one can. As a mortal human, you can have no idea how God will accomplish this great feat, but He has made it known through the Bible that He will. What you _do_ know is you have a part in the Lord's plan, the part that involves you and other believers spreading the Word, so don't think this discharges you from taking the Gospel to as many souls as you can. My 'Great Commission' still stands, and it's an important part of my Father's plan. But don't get all 'stressed-out' over the people you might miss, or who might not believe, or who have never heard the Word."

Jesus paused, seeing the concerned look on my face. "To answer your unspoken question: yes, there will be those who are not saved." Again he felt my concern. "I don't want you to obsess over the ones who may be lost. My Father knows about them, and all will be fulfilled according to His will in the end. So please," he implored, reflecting my own anxiety back at me, "_please_, stop worrying about it. It's under control. My Father is God for a reason you know."

I was excited about what I had discovered with my research and what Jesus had told me, so I called Matt back that very day. After I had relayed all of the information that was bursting out of me, Matt seemed impressed.

"Sounds like you really know what you're talking about Rob. And you're right: those old myths have been through a lot of revisions and additions over the ages. I'll have to check, but you may also be right that the 'resurrection' parts of the stories may have been added after the first century, which would mean they were added after the so called resurrection of Jesus. But I'm not sure I buy what you're saying about the exclusiveness of Christianity."

"Oh," I said cautiously. "Why is that?"

"Well, you may contend that most religions use some form of exclusiveness in their dogma, but that doesn't get Christianity off the hook. It's very obvious to me that you folks are always insisting the only way to be saved is to believe in Jesus Christ. But it also seems obvious that there have been, and always will be people who never even heard of Jesus or just weren't convinced when they did hear about him. There's no getting around the fact that, according to you people, those folks will burn in hell. Right?"

"Matt," I said after gathering my thoughts, "I'm just a man. A human person, nothing special. But so are the people who run religions and write the scriptures and make the rules. God is God. There's no one like Him. He <u>alone</u> is responsible for our salvation. Humans—people—don't have anything to do with it. If, as you say, there are those who haven't heard the Gospel, I have faith that it will somehow be communicated to them through the Holy Spirit. If, as you also say, there are people who have heard the Gospel, or parts of it, but don't believe it, then that's because they're using their brains and not their hearts; God can and <u>will</u> overcome this obstacle, I don't know how. But then, I don't have to understand it. I just have to accept it. Jesus died for the sins of the world. This is true whether you, or anyone else, believe it or not. This 'exclusiveness' you're talking about in Christianity was put there by man, not God. And I believe that God would not leave our salvation up to us alone. He is God after all, and if He wants someone to be saved, they'll be saved. And..." I was reaching to say what was in my heart. "No one is ever truly alone," I finally managed to say, my voice quivering slightly. "Jesus is always with us whether we know it or not. And God's saving grace is true whether we believe it or not." I was getting a bit choked up on the phone. There was a long pause.

I think I could hear Matt chuckling lightly on the other end of the phone. "Wow," he said. "Guess you told me! I'm proud of you Rob, for sticking up for your principles and your belief. I never meant to cast dispersions on your faith, you know that don't you?"

"Sure Matt. I know that. You have an open, inquiring mind, always searching for the truth. I don't think Jesus would have discouraged that kind of attitude. I just hope and pray that you will someday find faith enough to believe in the saving grace of God through Jesus Christ."

"We'll see ol' buddy…we'll see," he said.

Chapter Six: The Homeless Ones

My town, like others in the country, has its share of homeless: the disenfranchised who roam the streets, are seen frequently inebriated and/or prostrate on park benches and in doorways of stores, always present, always in need. I had often wondered about the homeless, how one finds oneself in such circumstances, how the difficulties in life can lead so many to the very bottom of the social order, with no home, no job, no car, few clothes, and even fewer prospects.

I was acquainted with two of these unfortunate people, a couple, Joseph and Marge. They had come to my church a few times in the past, looking for clothing and whatever hand-outs the church might have for such folk, and I had spoken with them for a little while each time I met them. This morning I saw them coming down the street heading into town, and when they saw me waving from my porch they started to come over. They were pushing an old grocery cart piled high with miscellaneous flotsam and jetsam they had gathered in their travels. Basically their sole possessions, all in that cart.

The two were not married, although they acted as if they were. I knew Marge had some mental health issues, but Joseph was a full-blown alcoholic who only went "on the wagon" when he had no money, which was most of the time since as soon as he had any he spent it on booze. Both Bob the Hat and I had tried to get Joseph to go to AA and try to quit the booze, but he was never interested. He and Marge actually preferred life on the street.

"There's the homeless couple I told you about," I whispered to Jesus as I waved them over to the porch. "I've talked to them a few times. They're coming over here, so let's see if they want to talk."

"Hey Rob," called Joseph, waving as he pushed the shopping cart over the curb and up to my porch. "How's life treatin' ya?" he asked as he and Marge stepped up to the porch railing.

"Hello Joseph...Marge," I said. "Going into town?"

"Yeah," said Joseph. "Gotta go see what's in the dumpster at the grocery store." Marge never said much; she just stood next to Joseph, her arm around his waist as if using him to prop herself up.

"The dumpster!" I cried. "That's disgusting! Why would you want to look in the dumpster for food?"

"Hey, there's a lot of good food in there. You'd be surprised what the stores throw away. Last week I made a fine vegetable stew for me and Marge that wasn't half bad."

"But you get food at the shelter, and the church has a free lunch program…and there are others organizations that distribute food. Why don't you go there?"

Marge was chuckling under her breath, but she still didn't say a word. "Haven't been back to the shelter in a while, not since I got kicked out for fighting the other night. And the church only serves hot dogs. Marge can't eat hot dogs," he said gesturing to the slender figure clinging to him.

"Fighting?" I replied. "Why were you fighting at the shelter?"

Joseph sighed. "Some [BLEEPER] was keeping Marge and me awake with his crazy chattering, so I told him to shut up. He didn't want to, so he took a swing at me. What could I do? I decked the [BLEEPER]!"

"And they immediately banned you from the shelter," I added.

"Yeah," he said. "So Marge and me are free-agents now. Sleeping on the bench in the park at night; good thing the weather's nice!"

"And the police don't hassle you?" I asked.

"Not too much, but sometimes they run us off, or take us in for the night."

"You mean jail? Have you been in jail recently?"

Marge started to laugh, lightly. You could hardly hear her.

"Hey, a night in jail is better than a night on the sidewalk," Joseph answered.

"But jail Joseph…that's not good. Why don't you try to get a job and then maybe you and Marge could get an apartment or something and you'd be on your way."

"On my way to where?" he asked.

"Well, on your way up…you know, up the social ladder. You can become a regular person. You know, working citizens."

Joseph shook his head vigorously and Marge mirrored the same motion. "Nope!" Joseph said. "To me 'work' is a four-letter word. Been there, done that…didn't like it. We like it better this way."

I was perplexed. I just didn't understand Joseph's reasoning. Why would a normal person (seemingly almost normal at least) prefer life on the fringe of society, living in the streets, with no job or home to stabilize them? It just seemed so contrary to the way life was supposed to be lived.

All this time Jesus had been sitting in his rocking chair, listening, but saying nothing. I looked over and gave him a "What do I say now?" look to cue him that I would like him to say something wise and edifying for Joseph.

"What?" Jesus asked.

"Aren't you going to contribute to this conversation?"

"What should I say?"

"You're asking me?" Apparently Jesus did not have much to say to Joseph and Marge.

"Who are you talking to?" Joseph asked, smiling a not-too-sure smile, as if he suspected I had too many birds on my antennae. So I explained about the chair for Jesus, and how each morning I sat on the porch and talked to him, and that he was sitting here right now listening.

"So what did he say?" Marge asked curiously, completely shocking me. It was one of the few times I had heard her speak a complete sentence.

"I haven't said anything yet," Jesus finally said. "What would you like me to say?"

I relayed Jesus' question to Marge.

"I'd like to hear him tell us our future," she said.

"No, you don't," Jesus responded immediately. "Besides, I don't do that. But anyone can see that your future is bleak unless you do something to turn it around."

I repeated the answer he gave to Marge, and her face dropped. I could see Joseph was annoyed.

"Just what does he mean by that?" Joseph asked pointedly.

I didn't need Jesus' help to answer. "Joseph, you know exactly what he means by that. You need a job so you can make money and get off the street."

"Well, he can forget about that!" Joseph replied, and started pushing his shopping cart back to the road.

I didn't want Joseph and Marge to go just yet. "Don't go Joseph, we're just trying to help."

"You call that help?" he said, pushing the cart back. "I've had jobs, all the good they did me. First I was laid off because of the [BLEEPING] economy, then the next job I got they fired me for being late, and then the next job…"

"Okay, okay," I interjected before he could continue. "I get it. You've had bad luck with employment. But that doesn't mean you should stop trying."

Joseph shook his head. "No, I've had it with going on interviews and punching the time clock and dragging myself out of bed every morning to do the same thing over and over again. And even with a job I still can't pay my bills. Me and Marge have to live in Section Eight housing and even that's not cheap, not to mention the electric and water bills, and the noisy neighbors…"

"Noisy neighbors!" I exclaimed. "You're complaining about noisy neighbors? You mean you prefer to sleep on a park bench?"

Joseph seemed insulted. "Hey man, it's pretty peaceful in the park at night, and you don't have to bang on the walls to get your neighbors to shut up. Don't knock it until you try it."

I had no idea what to say in response to that. "Well, okay, if that's the way you want it. But let me know if there's anything I can do to help."

"You wouldn't happen to have a cigarette on you?" Marge whispered.

"No. Sorry. I don't smoke. And neither does Jesus."

"Well then, okay, catch you later," Joseph said, and he and Marge pushed the cart back to the road to continue their trek to the Safeway dumpster.

After they left I turned to Jesus. "I really expected you to have a lot more to say to those two."

"Oh? How so?"

"I thought you'd have all sorts of advice for them. You know, I thought you'd say something to inspire them to get a decent job, better themselves…become like normal people."

"Rob, you know I hate it when you use terms like 'normal people.'"

Rats! I knew he'd jump on that, and I should've known better than to use a word like "normal" when I talk to Jesus. "Yeah, I know. But you understand what I mean, don't you? They're suffering, isn't it obvious?   They're homeless and miserable."

"They didn't seem all that miserable to me," he pointed out.

"You know what I'm talking about Jesus. Somebody needs to help them get back on track."

"I agree with you Rob," he said. "But first you have to determine if they want the help. And it appears that those two do not want the help. Why are you so concerned that they get jobs?"

"How else are they going to pick themselves up and get back to...get back on track?" I almost said the word "normal" again.

"And you don't think they need any other sort of help?"

"What do you mean?"

"You're so concerned with getting them a job that you may have missed something more basic. Why not start small? That way you won't offend them by trying to do so much, and they won't feel they owe you too much, and they also won't be overburdened by guilt."

"Guilt? What do you mean guilt?"

"Don't you think receiving so much help from others is a source of embarrassment to some people? If you help them with everything, especially the big things like getting a job, they could resent you for being so generous, and they might feel guilty that they couldn't do it for themselves."

"I don't know Jesus," I countered. "Seems to me that they don't have time for guilt. That's a luxury they certainly can't afford. And they need to do something about the way they're living. It's just not acceptable."

"Acceptable to whom?" he asked.

"Well, to society in general."

"Couldn't society be wrong? Or at the very least, couldn't society be mistaken in the case of those two?"

"I'm not sure what you mean," I said.

"Rob, the apostles and I were homeless. We had no permanent living place. We wandered from town to town, basically living on the charity of others. Don't you remember? 'Foxes have dens and birds have nests, but the Son of Man has no place to lay his head.' (Luke 9:58)."

I did remember that verse from Luke. "Okay, so if I can't help them find employment, what else can I do for them?"

"I didn't say you couldn't help them find employment, but you could also help to make life a little easier for them by helping them find food, clothing, temporary shelter… You can give them money, books, even TVs if you've a mind to… Just help them with the little things that makes life tolerable for all of you in these times."

"Okay," I said. "We can do those things. My church participates in Manna on Main Street, and clothes for the poor, and other assorted charities, but is this good enough?"

"I don't use terms like 'good enough' Rob, you know that. Just keep doing it until your heart tells you it's enough."

"But Jesus…I can't do it all alone. Sure, a lot of people from my church feel the same way, but there are a lot of people in this town and all through the country who resent the homeless and don't agree that helping them is a good thing. It just encourages homelessness they say. You'll just end up with thousands of needy people with their hands out…at least that's what some people say."

"'Truly I tell you, whatever you did for one of the least of these brothers and sisters of mine, you did for me' (Matt 25:40b),'" is all he said.

"But it just seems so pointless sometimes," I replied. "That's why I want to try to help them by getting jobs for them. You can give them clothes and food and stuff like that, but where does it lead? In the long run they're still homeless, still impoverished, still at the bottom of society. Where does it end?"

Jesus sighed. "Rob, existence is tough. All I'm saying is: do what you can. But it might be more helpful to start with the little things. And that goes for other projects as well. Maybe, instead of building that huge church building for the further glory of God why don't you try helping, just a little bit, the ones worse off than you? Instead of organizing a mega-church that pulls in millions of dollars, why not organize a food drive in your town?   Instead of buying that huge blue-ray HD monitor for your church why not start a separate church service at the homeless shelter?   Instead of standing in church repeating all the different ways you love me and my Father, why don't you show this love by helping the poor souls who need it, in all the little essential ways that really count?"

This caused me to think.   Maybe I could redirect my energies in humbler directions? Perhaps I could demonstrate my love for Jesus in other ways, through the needy and marginalized folks who would really appreciate help in this life, in this world, in these times. Instead of focusing on the next life, on Heaven, I should try to make life a little more "heavenly" for those who could use a boost, and hand up, which is much different from a "hand out."

"You've made me think about a lot of things I hadn't considered before," I told Jesus. "Perhaps I could drum-up some more help at the church for these people. Let me think about it and I'll bring it up at the next congregation meeting."

"That's all I'm saying," Jesus said, smiling that wonderful smile of his again.

Chapter Seven: The Keeper of the Law

I have a cousin, Johnny, who lives not far from here. He's a lawyer, and so is his wife Irene. He and Irene come by every now and then for a little visit. Last night they came by and we had dinner. Afterwards we talked. As usual the conversations broke up into men and women, and we separated into our pairs, my wife and Irene in the kitchen with me and Johnny in the living room. After the usual talk of cars and sports and other assorted masculine topics, our conversation touched on religion.

"You don't go to church much, do you Johnny?" I asked.

Johnny shook his head. "No, not much. Irene and I go sometimes, you know, at Christmas and Easter, or if someone gets married, or some other family religious function. But generally we don't go much."

"But you still consider yourself a Christian?"

Johnny nodded vigorously. "Sure I do. You don't have to go to church to be a Christian."

I thought that was a strange thing to say. "Why do you say that Johnny?"

"Well, if you keep the Ten Commandments and live a good life, why would you need to go to church?"

"To be around other Christians for one," I replied.

"Well sure, there's that," Johnny said. "But aside from that, all they want is your money."

"That's not true Johnny, you know that!"

Johnny laughed. "Sure it's true! The whole church thing is a scam!"

Now I knew he was baiting me. My stunned expression was too much for Johnny to take.

"Sorry man!" he laughed. "I was pushing your buttons."

"So you don't really believe it's a scam?"

"Well, yeah, I kind of do," he said slowly, becoming serious. "After they finish telling you how bad you are, how much of a low-life you are, how much you need them…they pass around the tray and ask for money. And they even keep track and let you know if you're not giving enough."

"The church doesn't tell you when you're not giving enough," I said defensively.

"Sure they do," Johnny said. "Ever hear of tithing?"

"Well, yeah." He was referring to the tradition of giving a tenth of one's earnings for the support of the church.

"There ya go," he said.

I thought for a moment. "But that's just a suggestion, a recommendation from the Bible. It's not a bill, not a rule. The Bible just recommends that we give ten percent of what we earn to the church. They don't care if you give less, just so you give what you can."

"Oh yeah? Tell that to the last church Irene and I belonged to a few years ago."

"I didn't know you ever belonged to a church?"

"Yes, we did," he affirmed. "Back when we were first married. Irene wanted to settle in, you know, community ties and all that. So we joined the local church. Then we didn't go for a while. I don't know…I was busy and Irene was visiting her mother or something, but we just didn't go for a while, maybe a month or two. Well, after a few weeks we got a phone call asking what had happened to us. I didn't especially want to talk to the deacon who called, so I gave him a quick excuse and left it at that. After a couple of weeks we got a notice in the mail: an <u>excommunication</u> notice!"

"A what?" I said, unable to believe what he said. "Excommunication" was an old concept used as a punishment for especially bad transgressions against the church. The church hierarchy effectively cuts the worshipper off from communion with the church and all its members. In the old days this meant certain damnation, for salvation apart from the church was unheard of back then, even unthinkable. I knew the Catholic Church sometimes used this penalty even today, although I was fairly certain they reserved it for special situations. I had never heard of any other Christian denomination using this old device however, and I was stunned to hear about it.

"Yeah, you heard me," Johnny said harshly. "They 'excommunicated' us for not paying our tithe, the amount we had agreed on when we became members of the church."

I told Johnny how astonished I was to hear of such a thing from a modern church. "I just can't believe they did that!" I lamented.

"Well they did, and ever since then Irene and I will never become a member of a church again."

"I'm so sorry you had such a bad experience with a church Johnny," I said to him. "But don't judge them all by one bad experience."

"Hey, water under the bridge. But we decided we didn't need church anyway. Like I said: if you keep the commandments and live a good life, don't kill anyone and don't cheat on your wife or on your taxes…you should be okay with God, right?"

"I don't know Johnny," I said while shaking my head, "I just don't know. But I'll let you know if I find out anything that might help."

"You do that Rob," he responded. We talked a bit more, and then Irene came out of the kitchen and they said their good-byes. Of course I had every intention of brining my conversation with Johnny up with Jesus the next morning.

"Good morning Jesus," I said as I walked onto the porch the next day, my coffee cup in hand.

"Good mornin' Rob." Jesus answered. "And how are you this morning?"

"I'm fine," I responded, then quickly got to the topic I wanted to bring up. "I wanted to talk to you about a conversation I had with my cousin Johnny last night."

"Okay," Jesus said. "Shoot!"

So I recapped my conversation with my cousin from the previous night to Jesus. When I had finished I waited for his response.

After a moment of two while Jesus absorbed what I had just told him, he spoke: "So which one of those polemics do you want me to comment on first: that all Christian churches want is your money, that a Christian doesn't have to go to church to be a Christian, or all you have to do is obey the commandments and live a good life?"

"All of them, but you can start wherever you'd like," I said.

"Okay, let's start with the money thing. You know I don't often comment on your man-made rules, right?"

"But the tithing rule comes from the Bible," I said. "I forget where it says it, but somewhere in the Bible is says you should give ten percent of your earnings."

"It's in the Old Testament," Jesus said. "In Leviticus 27 it says the law requires a tenth of all produce, flocks, and cattle to support the Levites, the priests back then. The same thing is repeated in the Book of Numbers. But really, I never used that old law. I just thought it was sufficient to ask my followers to give generously to those in need: 'Give to the one who asks you, and do not turn away from the one who wants to borrow from you. (Matt 5:42)'"

"But what about the Christian churches today that ask their members to tithe ten percent of their incomes?" I asked.

"I never tell the churches what they can and cannot do, especially when it comes to finances. The church needs a building, and a staff, and that requires maintenance and upkeep, so yes, they have to raise money from their members. But I never asked my disciples to give ten percent. As I said, that was an Old Testament law, back when they didn't have social services the way they do now. In the past they didn't have Social Security, Medicaid, food stamps, or assisted living and housing projects for the poor. No, in biblical times the only people who were taking care of the poor were the priests and the scribes in the Temple. That's why they needed ten percent, so they could care for the widows and orphans. You folks today, and especially in this country, have government sponsored social programs to take care of the needy, and the churches are only there to pick up the slack.

"But each church," Jesus continued, "each group of Christians has different needs. I would never presume to dictate to the churches how they run their finances, but it occurs to me that a well-organized church shouldn't need to require specific amounts of money from its members. They should plan their activities and then figure out how to reasonably fund those activities without putting undue stress on their members."

"But some churches, like mine for instance, can't plan for the year unless they get pledges from their members at the beginning of the year," I countered.

"So? Do they have to make pledges mandatory?"

"No, I guess not."

"And do they have to insist on ten percent?"

Again I had to agree with Jesus, they did not have to do that to come up with a workable yearly budget. Perhaps I should suggest to my pastor that we stop asking for "tithes" from our members and just ask that they give as much as they can.

"Something to think about, huh?" Jesus asked.

"Yeah. Okay, so how about the other one? About Christians going to church?"

Jesus pondered. "You know what I always say: Whenever there are two or more believers…"

"Yes," I answered. "'For where two or three gather in my name, there am I with them. (Matt 18:20).'"

"Right!" Jesus concurred. "So that means there has to be two or more, right? And why do you think I insisted that my disciples 'gather in my name'? Because you need each other! I know how hard it is to have faith, but it can be so much easier if you share your difficulties with fellow believers. This is the same for everybody who belongs to any kind of group. Whatever your group has in common, it's something that makes you a group unto yourselves. It's something the world in general doesn't provide, something that separates us from the world, like a team or a club. And it's not easy to hold a group together; sometimes it's difficult to hold onto the values that make your group a group. Coming together to share with like-minded people strengthens the group and helps the members to be firm in their values."

"So what you're saying is, Christians need to be with other Christians," I paraphrased.

"Yes, exactly!" Jesus said. "Christians need the support of each other, otherwise their faith may weaken, or they may lose their faith altogether if they're all alone."

"I'll be sure to point these things out to Johnny the next time I talk to him," I said.

"So now to your other issue," Jesus said. "So your cousin thinks that keeping the Ten Commandments and just living a 'good life' will make him okay with my Father, is that it?"

"Yeah, that's basically it. I hear that from a lot of people sometimes."

"You hear it!" Jesus exclaimed. "I've been hearing that argument for 2,000 years! And when the Reformation started it really got crazy. Everybody had their own opinion on what 'living a good life' meant."

"So that's why we have the Ten Commandments," I said.

"Right!" Jesus agreed. "But remember, those are just the top ten. There are over 600 other commandments in the Old Testament you know."

"But since we're Christians, according to Paul, we are not bound by those other commandments, just the Ten Commandments, right?"

"You mean the 'Ten Condemnants' don't you?" Jesus corrected.

"Condemnants?" I asked. "Why do you call them that?"

"Because nobody can keep them, so all they end up doing is condemning you."

"Why do you say nobody can keep them? Lots of people stick to the Ten Commandments. Some people want to post them in our courthouses, that's how much they respect them."

"Oh really," said Jesus. "They respect them but they can't keep them."

I was confused now. "Please explain," I asked.

"Tell ya what," Jesus said. "Let's take them in reverse order: 10. Coveting: Come on now! Your whole western culture is addicted to advertising, Madison Avenue, consumerism...all that stuff. It's the economic backbone of your civilization, or am I wrong? 9. Bearing False Witness: That's lying by another name... But everyone lies, right? It's only natural. Perhaps they're just those 'white lies,' right? And this commandment is a special case: <u>perjury</u>, a legal issue. The only way to condemn anyone for a crime back in the old days was to have a witness, and this commandment was to ensure the truth was told by witnesses. Even today you're not supposed to lie in court. But don't most people have their own agendas?"

I wanted to interrupt, but I knew better.

Jesus continued: "8. Adultery. The national pastime! And the most popular entertainment subject in your novels, movies, videos... Accepted behavior these days, no? Everybody's doing it! 7. Murder? We've already talked about that. <u>Raca!</u>

Anger, fear, spite, envy, jealousy, etc. 6. Stealing? Oh please! Everybody steals now and then, right? Pilfering pens at the office, taking towels from motels, etc. And that doesn't address the emotional robbery you folks do to one another every day."

I almost stopped Jesus to ask if he would clarify that last statement, but suddenly I knew what he meant: the psychological embezzling we do to each other on a daily basis, the supercilious lift we get from putting someone down or the feeling of superiority we experience when we correct someone. Basically the emotional bullying we unconsciously do to each other each day in the world we've created for ourselves.

Jesus went on. "5. Honor your parents: Nowadays a lot of seniors are treated like second rate citizens. Many sons and daughters leave their parents as soon as possible and never speak to them again. Still others put their elderly parents in homes and forget about them. Not much honor and respect there in a lot of cases. 4. The Lord's Day: And which day is that? Sunday? Saturday? Does it matter? These days they're even repealing the 'blue' laws so it's legal to sell liquor on Sundays. And how many go to church on The Lord's Day? To most people it's a day off, a day to sleep late, watch sports on TV and generally lay around. What the commandment is really saying is: take time for the Lord. But how many do that? 3. The Lord's name in vain: I've heard that some television networks are <u>not</u> censoring the "GD" word anymore, and they allow a lot of four-letter words too. Most people break this commandment so often they don't even realize they're doing it. 2. Graven Image: Oh, yeah…that's a popular one! And I'm not only talking about all the statues and paintings and what-not your culture likes to use in worship, but the other things you set up on pedestals and worship, like <u>television</u> or the <u>all-mighty dollar</u>. And then there's the BIG ONE…"

"Now hold on," I finally interrupted. I just had to say something at this point. "You're not going to say that people do not worship God as the <u>one and only</u> God, are you?"

Jesus smiled slightly, as he always does when he's about to make a point. "No, I wasn't going to say that, exactly."

"Well that's good." I felt relieved. "At least we got one out of ten."

"No. That one is never kept as well," Jesus said.

"What?"

"That's right! Think about it. The commandment says to have only the Lord God as your one and only God, right?"

"Yes," I agreed. "So?"

"So how many people can you think of who have another 'god' in their lives more important to them than the Lord?"

"I'm not sure I see what you mean," I admitted.

"I'm saying," he clarified, "that a lot of people these days have things in their lives that are more important to them than God. Just look around. An alcoholic might worship the bottle, a businessman might worship money, a sports fanatic often worships his home team, a young man might worship his sweetheart…the list is endless."

"But that's not having another god before the Lord, it's just…" I couldn't think of the phrase I was looking for.

"It's just the most important thing in their lives?" Jesus offered.

"Well, yeah, that's what I meant."

"Rob, the most important thing in your life is supposed to be God. Even putting your wife or husband or even your children before God is not a good replacement for the Lord. You must put God first in your life. That's why you were created. Everything falls into place if you have your priorities right."

"So you're saying most people don't even come close to keeping even one of the Ten Commandments?"

"I'm afraid so," he said sadly. "Nobody can keep them. That's why you need a savior."

"But we try," I lamented. "My cousin Johnny is a good man, and so is his wife, and I know they try to keep to the commandments."

"And that's very commendable, but they're fooling themselves if they think they can truly keep the commandments and be 'right with God.' Remember what I said about anger? Well, that goes for a lot of other sins as well. When you're angry with someone you're committing murder in your mind. It's that simple. Same with adultery. 'You have heard that it was said, do not commit adultery. But I tell you that anyone who looks at a woman lustfully has already committed adultery in his heart (Matt 5:27-28).'"

"Yes," I said. "I understand that."

"I was suggesting...and I'm suggesting right now...a new way, a different way...not the same old religion but a new <u>way of life</u>. And it all centers on your love of God and for each other." He paused briefly in thought. "Perhaps the best summary of this idea is in Matthew Chapter Five, verses 43-46: 'You have heard that it was said, love your neighbor and hate your enemy. But I tell you: Love your enemies and pray for those who persecute you, that you may be sons of your Father in Heaven... If you love those who love you, what reward will you get? Are not even the tax collectors doing that?'"

"So that's the kicker then, is it?" I asked.

"Yes, love your neighbor and receive God's grace. Everyone needs God's grace. Grace is superior to law because you are all law-breakers, in need of God's grace."

"But how do I explain that to Johnny?" I asked. I wasn't sure these Christian concepts would fly with my cousin.

Jesus thought for a moment. "Just tell him it all comes down to '<u>Agape</u>.'"

"Agape?"

"Yes," Jesus said. "One of the Greek words for love. <u>Agape</u>. You know: the selfless, sacrificial, unconditional love we have for one another. It always comes down to love."

"As I have always suspected..." I said playfully.

Chapter Eight: The Return of the Angry Man

It was Thursday morning and right on schedule, here came Bob the Hat, going into town for cigarettes. I called to him and waved him over to the porch.

He smiled as he came up to the porch. "Hey Bob! How's Jesus this morning?" He flicked the cigarette he was smoking to the curb. I guess he was back to calling me "Bob" again.

"Tell him I'm doing fine, thank you," Jesus said.

"He says he's doing fine, thanks," I told Bob.

Bob walked on to the porch and sat on the stool next to my chair. "I meant to tell you, the other day I tried out that little experiment you suggested."

"Oh really?" I said, surprised.

"Yeah. Just the other day when I came home from the Legion Hall, the [BLEEPING] dog had gotten into the [BLEEPING] trash again and dragged the whole [BLEEPING] thing all over the kitchen. There was garbage strewn all over the [BLEEPING] floor! I was so angry I was spittin' nails, but I remembered what you had said, and I thought I'd give it a try. So I laughed instead of cussin' the dog out."

"You laughed?" I could not quite believe what he said.

"Yeah, I started laughing like crazy. My ol' lady came into the kitchen when she heard me (must have thought I was [BLEEPING] nuts!) and then <u>she</u> started laughing with me. Pretty soon we were both rolling on the floor laughing. The dog was lookin' at both of us like we were bonkers!"

"Tell him I'm proud of him for exercising his free will," Jesus said.

So I told Bob we were proud of him. "Kind of proud of myself," he said. "It was fun, actually. Afterwards the wife and I cleaned up and went to a movie. We had a great evening for a change. No fighting or arguing like we usually do."

"See what happens when you resist evil," I said.

"Evil?" Bob said. "I was just mad at the dog for dragging the garbage all over the kitchen. That's not [BLEEPING] evil...it's just my bad temper."

"Even a bad temper can be considered evil," Jesus commented.

"That's right," I agreed. "Evil sometimes comes in small doses, inside our own hearts."

"That's not evil," Bob countered. "It's just bad. There are a lot of bad things in the world. But you don't have to call them [BLEEPING] evil."

"Anything that takes away from loving God and loving your neighbor is a form of evil," Jesus said.

When I told Bob what Jesus had said, he responded: "I'm not sure I agree with you there. The stuff I do is sometimes not good…maybe even [BLEEPING] bad, but I wouldn't call it evil."

"What would you call evil then," I asked.

"The 9/11 attack on the World Trade Center," Bob quickly replied. "Now that was [BLEEPING] evil!"

"Yes," Jesus agreed, "that attack was extreme evil, but there's a whole range of evil acts that people do every day. If we want to fight evil, we should first start with the evil in our own hearts."

I repeated this for Bob. "Is he trying to say I'm evil at heart?" he asked.

"No," Jesus answered, "I'm saying everyone is evil at heart. Oh, I know a lot of people like to think that humans are basically good, but that's simply not the case. Every person has an internal gyroscope that invariably leans toward the bad rather than the good. As Paul said, 'When I want to do good, evil is right there with me (Rom 7:21).'"

"So there are no good people, is that what he's saying?" Bob asked me. I looked toward Jesus.

Jesus laughed. "Everyone has some good in them, even if it's self-centered, but they also have sin deep inside them, that's what I'm also saying," he corrected. "Right from birth, even as children, the evil from Original Sin is obvious."

"Original Sin?" Bob asked. "I'm not up on all that [DARN] religious lingo you people use. What's 'Original Sin'?"

"It's the sin of Adam and Eve," Jesus explained. "When they rebelled against God and ate the forbidden fruit; that set the standard all people are born with: the spirit of rebellion."

"Okay," Bob said. "But even kids? How can kids be evil?"

I smiled at that, winking at Jesus. "Bob, don't you know the 'Toddler's Ten Commandments'?"

"Huh?" Bob seemed puzzled.

"Yeah, the 'Toddler's Ten Commandments.' It goes something like this:

"1. If I like it, it's mine.

"2. If it's in my hand, it's mine.

"3. If I can take it from you, it's mine.

"4. If I had it a little while ago, it's mine.

"5. If it's mine, it must never appear to be yours in any way.

"6. If I'm doing or building something, all the pieces are mine.

"7. If it looks like mine, it's mine.

"8. If I saw it first, it's mine.

"9. If you are playing with something and you put it down, it automatically becomes mine.

"10. If it's broken, it's yours."

Bob was laughing by the time I finished the list. "That's just being selfish," he said chuckling.

"And being selfish is bad, right?" Jesus asked.

"Well, yeah, sure. I guess so," Bob said.

"Well, my Father does not distinguish between bad and evil, between anger and murder, and neither should we. Whenever we turn from my Father's ways we reveal our true nature."

"And our true nature is evil, because of Original Sin, is that right?" I said.

"Right, your original nature that you were born with has evil in it. But I know many people can't stomach that idea. The humanists would tell you just the opposite: that people are actually good at heart and just need the right conditions for that goodness to come out. But if that's true, how can we explain the horrible mess we find the world in today?"

"I hear that," Bob concurred.

"Why," Jesus asked, "do you think it's so hard to forgive but easy to begrudge? Why is faith so difficult but disbelieving so easy? Why do we have a hard time praising folks but find it very easy to criticize them? Why is it so hard to give generously to the poor, but easy to ignore them? No, to follow me you need to change your heart and become a new person, a God-person. And the only real way people can fight evil is with my Father's help."

"And we do that by believing in you, right?" I added.

"That's where it starts," Jesus said. "But it doesn't end there. No, believing is just the start of your spiritual journey. If you want to fight evil you must start with what's in your own heart, where the evil is so deeply ingrained that you really need to replace your old heart with a new one and start over."

"We have to be 'born again'" I added.

"Yes!" Jesus said. "'You should not be surprised at my saying, you must be born again. (John 3:7)'"

Bob was trying to take this all in, I think, but he had reached his limit. "Oh, there you guys go again, with the 'born again' [CENSORED] and that religious stuff."

"It's God's gift to you," I said. "A new heart. 'If anyone is in Christ, he is a new creation; the old has gone, the new has come! (2 Cor 5:17)"

Bob was dubious. "What happens if I want to make do with my old heart?"

"Your choice," Jesus said. "But if you've got things in your life you want to correct, it's the only way to go about it." Then he paused. He wanted to ask something. "Bob, do you have a computer?"

"What?" The question surprised Bob. "A computer? Sure, I have a PC, for all the good it does me."

"Gives you some trouble?" Jesus asked.

"[BLEEPING] right!" Bob exclaimed. "Thing's always breaking down, error messages all the time and all that [BLEEPING] spam garbage. The other day I couldn't even shut it down; had to pull the plug, and that probably made it [BLEEPING] worse!"

"Maybe you need to reload a new operating system?" Jesus suggested.

"I did that last year," I interjected. "My laptop started giving me trouble, so I loaded the next version of the operating system, and it was fine after that."

"Yeah," Bob agreed. "Maybe that's what I should do."

"That's right," Jesus said. "And that's what I'm talking about. This is what my Father can do for you: reinstall a new operating system, a Christian operating system, one that will recognize evil in all its forms and work against it."

"Sort of like anti-computer virus protection?" Bob speculated.

"Precisely!" Jesus agreed.

"So you think I need to reload myself?" Bob asked.

"Yes, I think you do," Jesus confirmed. "When we allow my Father to work inside of us, our moral guidance system works correctly, pointing to good and not bad. Every time you ask for forgiveness from God you're asking Him to do His work in you, recreating you anew, wiping out the old evil heart and reinstalling a new, good heart."

"Okay," Bob said. "I'll work on it. But that's just me. How will this help fight against all the evil—the <u>big</u> evil—of the world?"

"Well, working on yourself will help a lot to fight the evil that constantly surrounds us, the fraud, the deceit, the corruption, the hatred, the emotional and physical pain we inflict on one another all the time. And in this way you can begin to fight against oppression, torture, genocide, murder, rape, terrorism, sexual and physical abuse, neglect, injustice…the list goes on and on. But you have to start with yourself first."

Bob sat silently for a second. "Okay. Makes sense. I'll see what I can do," he said.

"Hey Bob!" I quickly added before he could leave. "Do you want to come to church with me and Lucy next Sunday?"

"Let me ask my wife and I'll let you know," he said, looking at his watch. "Well, better get to the store so I can start my day. Have a good one!"

"Thanks! See you later," I said.

Once Bob had walked down the street Jesus turned to me. "I do believe Bob's language has gotten better Rob."

"I think you're right Jesus," I agreed.

Chapter Nine: The Buddhist

It was Tuesday, and once again I was at the grocery store for my weekly shopping (since I'm unemployed and home most of the time I decided I would do the food shopping for us during the week until I got a job, instead of us going shopping together on the weekend). While I was shopping I bumped into a woman I knew from a while back. She used to come to our church regularly but I hadn't seen her in a couple of months.

"Hi Nancy!" I said as I pushed my grocery cart up to hers.

"Oh, hi Rob," she said, surprise on her face. "How are you?"

"Just fine Nancy; long time no see."

She seemed a little embarrassed. "Yeah, I haven't been back to church in a while. Had a little crisis with my ex-husband, but things have calmed down since then. But I have a new direction: I'm a Buddhist now!"

I knew Nancy had been divorced from her husband for a few years, with one child that her husband had custody of but she still saw every other week. I wasn't sure what crisis she was referring to, and I was equally unsure if I really wanted to know the details.

"A Buddhist!" I said. "Wow!"

"Well, not really a full-fledged Buddhist," she admitted. "But I'm studying, and I have an ex-monk helping me at the Buddhist temple downtown."

"What made you want to become a Buddhist?" I asked. I'll admit I was disappointed that she would not be coming back to our church, but I was happy for her; she seemed less anxious then I remembered.

"Well," she began, "I had a hard time with my divorce...I think I mentioned that to you once. I went through a serious depression, had to see a doctor and take anti-depressants, it was pretty bad. Then I met this ex-monk who turned me on to Buddhism and loaned me some books; after I read them I was extremely interested in this Buddhist religion, so I signed up for some classes at the temple and my friend is helping me to understand the Eight Fold Path of Buddha and how I can eliminate desire."

I had read-up on Buddhism myself some years ago, when I was in college, and it <u>is</u> fascinating, but I was never really captivated by it as a religion.

"From what I know about Buddhism it appears to be more of a philosophy than a religion," I said. "I mean, there's no priests or rabbis, no sacraments, no liturgy that I'm aware of…I don't even think they talk about God at all."

"I'm not sure I can reply to that," she said carefully. "You're right, they don't have those things. But it's given me some hope and relief from the pressures of life, and that's really all I ever wanted from any religion."

"And you didn't get any of that from our church," I asked sadly. Her face began to redden, and I realized I had embarrassed her. "Hey, I'm sorry, I didn't mean to put you on the spot," I apologized. "But I'm really curious to know what you got from Buddhism that you couldn't get from Christianity."

She thought a second and then said: "Inner peace."

Inner peace? I couldn't hide the surprise on my face. "You felt no inner peace when you were going to our church?"

"I'm sorry Rob," she lamented. "I just couldn't warm up to Christianity. I've had that feeling all my life, that there was something missing from my spiritual life, and I just couldn't find it in the Christian church. I'm afraid I just didn't have the kind of faith it takes to believe."

This disturbed me. I told Nancy I was happy for the inner peace she seemed to have found in Buddhism; I extended her a perpetual invitation to come back to our church anytime she wanted, and we said our good-byes.

As I was driving back home from the grocery store I passed the library where I had done all that research the other day. I decided to drop in and find a book on Buddhism, just to refresh my knowledge of Buddha and the so-called religion he started.

I found a couple of books on Buddhism and one on the life of Siddhartha Gautama, the real name of the original Buddha, who began to teach his new philosophy about 500 years before the birth of Jesus.

Apparently Buddha's religion was basically a method of removing desire, which the Buddha came to understand was the cause of human suffering. Basically, the Buddha hypothesized, if you could eliminate desire you could eliminate the suffering and pain people experienced in life. It seemed a noble ideal, but as far as I could see the Buddha never talked of divine matters, never mentioned God or Heaven or anything familiar to western religions such as Christianity and Judaism. His was a "sitting" religion, with much emphasis on meditation to still the mind and achieve spiritual bliss. I could see where the attraction was for Nancy and others like her. It seemed to be more practical than other mainstream religions. It addressed suffering directly.

The next morning I brought this up to Jesus.

"Good mornin' Jesus."

"Good mornin' Rob," said Jesus from the rocking chair. "How are things for you this morning?"

I told him about my conversation with Nancy, and how I then went to the library and did a little research on Buddhism.

"And what did you find out?" he asked.

So I explained what I had discovered about Buddhism at the library. "Did you and the apostles know of Buddhism?" I asked when I had finished.

'We knew of it," Jesus answered. "But we didn't know much about it. Since Jerusalem and the whole country for that matter was on the trade route between the east and west we had many travelers from the east come through; of course we heard stories from them about the Buddha and his religion, just as we heard stories about the Hindu religion and the Zoroastrian religion and all those mystery cults from the east. Sometimes I would discuss these stories with my disciples, but I always felt there really wasn't much substance for my disciples to use in those stories. It was eastern mysticism, and to Jews at that time that meant occult practices, forbidden by God. Although there was much the Buddha taught that was true, I could not detect the kind of Truth, the knowledge and awe of the Most High, in what I heard about Buddhism. And I wanted to give my disciples the Truth, with a capital 'T.'"

I was surprised to learn the disciples actually knew about other eastern religions, but I guess I shouldn't have been surprised. As my friend Matt had pointed out, the area where Jesus lived and preached was a hot-bed of foreign travel and trade, and the disciples would have known about the rest of the world, almost as well as we do today.

"What I found out was that the religion Buddha started was more of a philosophy, really," I said. "He seemed to be more concerned with the way people felt, about the stress of life in general, than he was about the afterlife or even God. His main message seems to have been the elimination of human desire to lessen the amount of suffering people experienced in life."

"I can't really fault him for that," Jesus admitted. "In a way, there's a correlation between Buddhism and the Tree of Knowledge in the Garden of Eden."

"Oh, how so?" I asked.

"The Tree of Knowledge was forbidden to Adam and Eve because it would impart to them certain 'knowledge' that God didn't want them to have. Now, what was this 'knowledge' you might ask? It can't be the regular knowledge we associate with that word, such as knowledge of God, because Adam and Eve at the beginning were very close to God: they 'walked' with God. No, it was a different kind of knowledge my Father was trying to keep from them: the <u>knowledge of desire</u>. Before they ate from the Tree of Knowledge they did not know they were mortal: that they would one day face death. They did not know they needed to feed and clothe themselves. They knew nothing of shelter or protection and they didn't even realize they were naked. They were in a state of blessedness where nothing mattered but being in the Garden and being with God. They had no desire for anything but God. In a way they were in a perpetual state of bliss. They had been made already enlightened. However, once they ate of the fruit from the Tree of Knowledge they suddenly realized they needed clothes, they needed to feed themselves, and that meant finding food (my Father would no longer provide it ready for them to pick from the trees), they needed to protect themselves from the elements, and once there were other people in the world…from each other! They had lost their bliss. They discovered the world outside the Garden (for they had been evicted from the Garden) was dangerous and forbidding."

"And they hadn't realized that before," I asked.

"No," Jesus answered. "They had no knowledge of these things, things we know of well today. They had been living in the state of mind Buddhism appears to be trying to reach. But once they disobeyed and lost their connection with God, all they had left were <u>material pleasures</u> and the desire for those things which they hadn't experienced before they ate the fruit. This was the knowledge my Father was trying to keep from them. It wasn't so much a Tree of Knowledge as it was a 'Tree of Human Desire': the desire for pleasure and worldly comfort. The Buddha maintained that to reach enlightenment you have to eliminate desire. Well, that seems to be the very thing my Father in Heaven was trying to keep from Adam and Eve. But because of free will, He was unsuccessful, as we know."

"I hadn't thought about that," I said. "So there are things that Christianity and Buddhism have in common?"

"It would seem so," Jesus agreed.

I would have to make a mental note of this comparison so I could tell Nancy about it. "Anyway," I continued, "the story goes that he was born an Indian prince, rich and prosperous, and he lived in luxury at the beginning of his life. Then he saw a dead man in the street and was overwhelmed with compassion. He became an ascetic, and went about the country begging in rags and fasting, until he reached what's been called 'enlightenment.'"

"I can relate to that compassion he felt," Jesus said. "But he reacted differently than I."

"True," I agreed. "But after he achieved this enlightenment, because he was so filled with compassion for his fellow suffering humans, he started communicating to his followers how they could go about achieving the same thing. He developed a program called 'The Eight Fold Path' and started teaching people how to meditate and eliminate desire from their lives. The aim of his spiritual program was the complete elimination of suffering and stress."

"You know," Jesus pondered, "it occurs to me that if suffering were a sickness, the Buddha's program for easing suffering by eliminating desire would be like an anesthetic to deaden the pain, not really a cure for the sickness."

"That occurred to me too when I was doing my research. Like when you're injured and you go to the hospital, they first give you something to deaden the pain; then they go to work on what's causing the pain. Buddhism seems to be only a pain-killer. The Buddha was mainly concerned with retreating from this world to avoid all the suffering. His 'Eight Fold Path' hardly addressed the actual cause of the suffering. He was more focused on the elimination of pain."

"Yes," Jesus said, "and I never heard anything in the stories about his religion having a personal relationship with any deity, not even the ancient gods of India. His religion was basically nontheistic. The Buddha never concerned himself with sin, or repentance or forgiveness or any of the familiar concepts of western religion. I don't think he prayed to any deity either, if he prayed at all. To me and my disciples it seemed a rather impersonal religion."

I had to agree, it seemed impersonal to me too. Originally there were none of the trappings of western religion associated with Buddhism, but as the centuries rolled on the followers added to the religion, and there became two branches of Buddhism: Theravada and Mahayana, with their own separate ideas, methods and philosophy for achieving a state of bliss. In the centuries that followed the Buddhists added worship of "worthy ones" who achieved enlightenment, as well as worship of what was called the "Eternal Buddha." Added to this were statues of Buddha and other relics that became objects of worship; so today most Buddhists perform some kind of worship or ceremony in their "service," although a westerner would hardly recognize it as such.

"I keep trying to figure out why so many people find Buddhism so attractive," I said. "I know a lot of folks are seeking peace and truth in their lives, but they have a hard time finding it in today's world."

"You know," Jesus said, "I've observed that many people today do not believe there is absolute Truth. They think truth is relative to whatever cultural attitude is current at the time. Some think one person's idea of truth is subjective and not useful for others. What seems good _is_ good, what seems right _is_ right.   But if everything is valid, then nothing is valid. Everyone paints their own picture of God, making God to be just like them. Actually, religion is mostly treated as another branch of the arts, like styles and fads that come and go, hub-caps or not, stripes or plaids?"

"You think that's the case with Buddhism?" I asked.

"Rob, I would never criticize a religion, or philosophy if you like, that has been such a comfort and a salvation of sorts for so many people through the ages. But I don't think it answers the important questions."

"Like why are we here and for what purpose," I suggested.

"Precisely," he said. "You're right when you say that people are seekers, and they seek the truth, but I do not believe it is useful to declare that there is no real truth. I believe in telling people the Truth."

"And the Truth is…" I hinted.

A smile crossed Jesus' lips. "You want to know the Truth Rob? Okay, here's what you need to know: there <u>is</u> a God, and you're <u>not</u> Him (that's important). The other truth you need to know is: God <u>loves you</u>. And He wants you to <u>spend eternity with Him</u>. The way you reconcile yourself to God, for you are a fallen being, <u>is through me</u>. I am God's love in physical form. And that's the Truth."

"But people get so confused sometimes," I said. "They seek, but they don't find. They knock, but nobody answers. So they seek some more until they find some relief."

"Maybe they're asking the wrong questions," Jesus suggested. "Maybe their seeking in the wrong places, knocking on the wrong doors…"

"But it's so hard to decide which way is the right way," I lamented.

"'If you don't know where you're going, any road will get you there.'" I looked at him a bit perplexed. He smiled and winked. "Ancient Chinese saying," he said.

Chapter Ten: The Investor

My father called the other day and he was upset. Since he retired he's taken to dabbling in the stock market, and he's very conscious of his investments and how well they're doing, or how badly. Apparently the stock market was not doing very well these days.

"I'm tellin' you Rob," he was saying over the phone, "the bottom's fallen out of the market! It's taken a plunge of over 500 points. Most of my stocks have lost over 13% or more."

"It isn't that bad, is it Dad?" I asked innocently. I did not dabble in stocks because my wife and I lack the one prerequisite you need: discretionary funds. We were always broke. Not "poor." I never use that word. We weren't poor: we were rich in the spirit; we lived life to the fullest through the grace of our Lord God. We were just broke most of the time. But it's only money.

"I tell you the market is in free-fall. There's no bottom. It's starting to look like 1929 all over again!"

My father could be rather dramatic at times. "I'm sure it's just temporary Dad," I consoled. "The market will probably recover in a few days, and you'll be back on top again."

"Oh yeah," he countered. "Well, let me tell you something. People are trying to sell stocks right now, but nobody's buying. Billions of dollars are being lost. My portfolio manager said we have a situation where panic and fear have overwhelmed greed."

Really? Panic and fear have overwhelmed greed? That was extraordinary in today's world! But it reminded me of what a powerful emotion fear was. Fear can turn us away from God. It can cause us to forget our faith in God's saving grace through Jesus Christ. The turmoil of the world can get you down sometimes...really down.

I brought this topic up with Jesus the next morning. "It really gets to me when I hear about people who are so fearful, so afraid," I explained to him. "And what they're afraid of is losing their money. Just losing their money."

Jesus nodded. "Money is very important to a lot of people," he said sadly.

"That's an understatement," I replied. "Lately, with the advent of the Internet, regular folk are getting online and buying stocks, like my dad. It's almost like online gambling. But it gets scary sometimes. And what seems to frighten people most is…becoming a person like me who's broke most of the time, living paycheck to paycheck. There are people jumping out of windows because they can't bear the thought of becoming like me. Now what does that say about me?"

"Well, it says to me that you've got your priorities straight," Jesus replied. "Those who invest should be prepared to lose their money as well as make some money. If they invested thinking they'd become rich I guess this time they were disappointed."

I appreciated what Jesus was saying, and he was probably saying it as a comfort to me since I often lamented about not being able to invest in stocks and such. But my wife and I never emphasized money, or material gain; we both agreed we wanted to avoid the stress and anxiety that sometimes comes with disposable wealth and heavy investments. "It just astonishes me how many people, especially in America, think money equals happiness."

"It's an old story," Jesus said. "Some people can't see that happiness does not depend on having a pot of gold, despite what the fairytales might say."

"As a matter of fact," I said, "from what I remember of those old fairytales, a pot of gold is just as likely to bring unhappiness as anything else. Why can't people see that?"

"You said it yourself: fear. They're fearful, and they see money as the great fear-reliever. If they have enough money, the theory posits, they can keep unhappiness at bay."

"Yeah, but that's only for the problems that can be solved with money."

"Rob, any problem that can be solved with money is <u>not really a problem</u>."

That statement gave me pause, so he elaborated further.

"Real problems," he said, "the kind that destroy life's happiness, cannot be solved with money. Hardships such as death, addiction, unfaithfulness, desertion…<u>cancer</u>. Think of all the money they've raised for cancer research over the years, yet an actual cure is still far off. Money cannot solve everything."

"But folks still believe that if they have enough money they can keep those things out of their lives. They're so wrong," I mourned.

"And they don't seem to know they can lay their problems before my Father in Heaven," Jesus added. "'Do not be anxious about anything, but in everything, by prayer and petition, with thanksgiving, present your requests to God (Philip. 4:6).'"

"Why do you think that is, Jesus?"

"They're minds are on earthly things and not on the things that really matter," he said.

The New Testament says that very thing in Colossians 3:1-2: "Since, then, you have been raised with Christ, set your hearts on things above, where Christ is seated at the right hand of God. Set your minds on things above, not on earthly things." And I knew he was right. Too many of us become so preoccupied with the "stuff" of this world and the tangled ways of this high-tech life we live that we never realize there's a better way. A way to function in the world, sure, but also a way to keep your eye on the prize: a boundless relationship with the Lord of the Universe.

"I just wish I could make people like my dad understand there are more important things in life than just making a load of money," I said.

"Well, maybe you have to tell them without letting on that you're telling them," he said astutely. "Try allegories and metaphors, ones he might understand." Then he had a thought. "You know, it occurs to me that the email you received from your friend the other day, you know…the one you showed me about the buzzard, the bat and the bumblebee… That might serve to get the message across in some way."

I knew which email he was talking about, so I immediately went to my laptop and called up my inbox. I found the email from my friend immediately, opened it up and began reading it aloud.

"A bumblebee," I began, "if dropped into a jar, will stay there until he dies unless he is taken out. He never sees the way to escape at the top of the jar; he keeps trying to find some other way out through the sides of the jar near the bottom. He will seek a way out when there is none, until he dies.

"If you put a buzzard in a stall," I continued, "say eight-feet square, that is open at the top, the buzzard, despite its ability to fly, will not be able to get out. Why? Because a buzzard always takes off from the ground by running about 10 feet or more. Without the space to run it will not even attempt to fly, but will remain a prisoner for life in a small jail with no top.

"You've seen bats before," I read from the email, "and you've seen how they fly around at night, remarkably nimble, right? But that's in the air. A bat cannot take off from a level place. If it's placed on the floor or flat ground, all it can do is squirm around helplessly until it reaches some little elevation where it can throw itself into the air. Then it soars like a bird!"

As I finished reading I looked up at Jesus, who sat attentively in his chair smiling. "So people are just like the buzzard, the bat, and the bumblebee," I concluded. "They struggle all the time with their problems and frustrations, never realizing that all they have to do is look up to God in Heaven for all the answers they'll ever need."

"Correct!" Jesus said. "That's one way to illustrate the concept."

I had forgotten about this email, and I was glad Jesus reminded me of it. I liked the way the analogies came together. "Why is it so hard to get people to see that," I asked.

"We've already answered that question: fear," Jesus reminded me. "Fear is a powerful motivator for most people, in all cultures, throughout history. In ancient times they feared for their lives...starvation, disease, imprisonment, execution, murder... These days it's the same, really, only the things people fear are a bit different: powerlessness, poverty, boredom, loss of status...and self-image. But it's still fear, just over different things. In the old days I saw fear in the faces of the apostles all the time."

"So not much has changed since then."

"No, just the things you fear. That's why there's faith. Faith is the only true way to fend off fear. I tried very hard to get that message across to my disciples. I remember," Jesus reminisced, "when the apostles and I were out in a boat on the

Sea of Galilee and a storm came upon us. I was tired from preaching all day and I was taking a nap in the bow of the boat when the storm hit. It totally terrified the apostles, so they tried to wake me up. I didn't want to wake up, so I stayed where I was. Now, you'd think they'd let me rest and not worry about the storm since they were with me, but no! They continued to try to wake me up. 'Teacher, do you not care that we are perishing?' they asked me (Mark 4:39). So I got up—a little grumpy I'll admit—shouted at the wind like King Lear and yelled 'Quiet! Be still!' and the sea calmed right away."

"I'll bet that shut them up," I laughed.

"Oh yeah," Jesus said. "Then I got all over them for waking me up. I wanted to know two things: first, why were they afraid when they were with me? And second, how could it be that after all we had been through together, they still had such little faith?"

"What did they say to that?" I asked.

"Oh, the usual, how they worried the boat would capsize and drown us all, how they thought there was something wrong with me because I was sleeping so soundly, the usual things. They were such worriers."

"And you always had a lot to say about worrying, didn't you?" I said. "I remember one quote: 'Who of you by worrying can add a single hour to his life?' (Matt 6:27)."

"Very good," Jesus said, smiling. "And don't forget my favorite: 'Therefore do not worry about tomorrow, for tomorrow will worry about itself. Each day has enough trouble of its own (Matt 6:34).'"

"Oh yeah!" I quickly agreed. "That's one of my favorites too!"

Chapter Eleven: The Cracked Pot

I had a job interview some miles away, and it was close to a town where a friend of mine lives, so I decided to drop by for a visit. I called before I went over to make sure Mike was home, and then I drove to his address.

Mike was a strange guy. When I met him at college he was majoring in Philosophy. I remember asking him what kind of job he thought he'd get with a degree in Philosophy and he had answered: "I don't know…stand-up comedian?" That gives you an idea as to what kind of guy Mike was. He had a great sense of humor though.

Unfortunately he never took anything very seriously, and that included his studies. His parents had paid his way through college, unlike me. I had to take out loans to pay for my college tuition. Maybe that's why I took my studies more seriously than Mike. Just in the short time I knew him he changed his major three times! I think he finally settled on Radio & Television Production, but I'm not sure if he ever got his degree.

When I got to his house I was surprised to see two broken-down cars in the front yard, the grass overgrown and uncut, and the front siding on the house badly in need of a paint job; the screen on the front door was held on by one hinge as it tangled precariously in the wind. I pushed it aside and knocked on the battered old wood-panel door. My knock echoed through the old house.

Mike came to the door in his bathrobe. "Hey Rob!" he bellowed as he opened the door. I was happy he was glad to see me. He was unshaven and looked like he just got out of bed. It was three o'clock in the afternoon.

"Hi Mike," I said as he opened the door and let me in. "It's been a long time. You look like you just woke up?"

"Nah," he said, "just didn't have anything to get dressed for today, so why not stay in your PJs, huh?"

Mike always had been a bit of a lay-about. Back in college he used to sleep in and miss most of his morning classes. After a while he got wise and only signed up for afternoon classes. I guess Mike's the type of person who doesn't make the extra effort to be successful. To Mike, if something didn't come to him easily, like a job or an opportunity, then he wasn't that interested. I remember whenever we did anything together back in college, Mike always had to be talked into it. He didn't initiate activity on his own.

"So what've you been up to these days Mike?" I asked as I finally found a chair that was not covered in debris to sit on.

"No much," was his reply. "Just the same ol' same ol'."

I wasn't going to let him cop-out on me as he always did in the past when I asked him a question like this. "You know," I said, "I'm not sure I even know what the same ol' same ol' is, or used to be."

"I hear ya!" he laughed.

"No, I'm serious," I said. "I don't think I ever knew what you did for a living Mike."

Mike blinked a few times as if he didn't understand my question. "Oh heck man, I thought you knew," he finally said. "I write a blog online, 'Mike's Mike,' it's a take-off on an open microphone. I post blogs about current affairs, my views on things, you know, that sort of thing…"

Sounded a bit half-baked to me. "And you make real money doing that?" I asked.

"Well, not a heck of a lot, that's for sure," he said. "I also sell things on eBay, to make up the cash."

"Whatever happened to television producing?" I asked.

"What? Oh, that never panned out. Tried to get into that after graduation, but I didn't know the right people."

"Right people?"

"Yeah," he answered. "If you don't know the right people, you can't get into television or radio."

I wasn't sure if that was true, but I didn't want to challenge him on it. "Ever think of getting a real job?" I asked.

"What d'ya mean a real job," he replied, feigning insult. "I have a real job! Blogging's a legitimate job. I make good money blogging."

"But you just said you have to sell things on eBay to make more money," I countered.

"My eBay business is a side-line, and both of those together make enough for me to afford this place," he gestured to our surroundings.

While I didn't want to comment on the quality of his abode, I did think that Mike could do better. When I had known him he was a really smart guy. A little lazy perhaps, but smart. He could do so much more with his life.

"I don't know Mike," I said, "I think you could do so much better."

"Better than what?" he asked.

"Better than this place, and those jobs," I said. "Mike, you're a smart guy, with a college degree. Wouldn't you like to have a better house to live in? Wouldn't you like to settle down someday with a wife and kids maybe?"

"Are you kidding?" he asked.

"No, I'm not."

His face screwed up, as if he had just bit into a grapefruit. "Rob, I am perfectly happy living the life I live right now. And no, I have no ambition to shackle myself to a wife and bring little rug-rats into the world. Who would want to have kids these days anyway, with the world as it is? And as far as a career goes…no, I've tried corporate America, and I didn't like it. Nothing but money-grubbing phonies in the offices of this country these days, if you ask me. Office politics, back-stabbing and game-playing; who needs it?"

He did seem to know what he wanted, or rather didn't want. Who was I to argue with him? So we talked for a little while, and eventually I was on my way back home after telling Mike we should get together some evening so he could meet my wife.

But my visit with Mike troubled me, and I brought the subject up the next morning with Jesus.

"Good morning Jesus."

"Good mornin' Rob." Jesus said. He was sitting with his eyes closed again, experiencing the moment.

I immediately told him about my visit with Mike the day before. "So what do you think?" I asked when I had finished.

"About what?" Jesus asked.

"About my friend Mike," I supplied. "Is there any way you can think of that I might spur him on to better things?"

"Better things?" Jesus asked quizzically.

"Yeah," I said, "you know…a better life. A better job, so he can afford a better house. He lives in a shack for cryin' out loud, in filth with junked cars in his front yard."

"Did he say he wanted a better life?" Jesus asked.

"Not in so many words," I said. "But you could tell he just wasn't happy in the state of things."

"Are you sure?" Jesus said. "Or did you just take it for granted that he would want to better his circumstances?"

I was bewildered. Yet he was right. Mike did not say anything to indicate he was unhappy. I decided that for myself. Was I wrong?

"But you should have seen his place," I said to Jesus. "It was a dump! And he was in his bathrobe! He probably didn't get dressed all day!"

"And that's bad?" Jesus asked.

"You bet it's bad!" I said. But then I had a second thought. Again, was I jumping to conclusions?

"Rob, you seem to think that anyone who isn't living life the same way you are is unhappy and needs to change, but that's just not true. The world is made up of all kinds of folks."

I knew that. Did I really need the Prince of Peace to be telling me something so obvious? "I know that," I told Jesus. "But I just can't seem to leave it alone. I mean, does Mike contribute to society? He's writing online blogs, and I know you can't make much money writing those! Shouldn't he be using his considerable brain to do more marketable things, things that pay better than blogging, so he can buy better clothes and a better house? Who doesn't want these things?"

"Apparently Mike doesn't want them," Jesus answered.

"Okay," I said. I could tell I was losing my argument. So I thought I'd use a different line of reasoning. "What possible use could God make of him? I mean, he's dysfunctional. He's of no use to anyone, including God."

"That's where you're dead wrong Rob," Jesus said.

Wrong? I was wrong? About which part? "How am I wrong?" I asked.

"You're wrong if you think my Father can't use such people," he said.

"How so?" I asked.

"Have I ever told you the parable of the cracked pot?" Jesus asked.

"No, I don't believe so…"

"Okay…" he said. "A water bearer had two large clay pots that hung on the end of a long pole across his neck that he used to carry water. One of the pots had a large crack in it, but the other pot was perfect and always delivered a full measure of water at the end of the long walk from the stream to the master's house. But the cracked pot was only half full at the end of the trip.

"This went on daily for two years, with the water bearer delivering one and a half pots of water for his master every day. The perfect pot was quite proud of itself for its accomplishments, being perfect to the end for which it was made. But the cracked pot was ashamed of its imperfection, and saddened that it was able to accomplish only half of what it was made to do.

"So, after two years of what it considered to be terrible failure it spoke to the water bearer one day by the stream. 'I am ashamed of myself, and I want to apologize to you,' it said.

"'Why?' asked the water bearer. 'What are you ashamed of?'

"'Because of this crack in my side,' the cracked pot said, 'that causes water to leak out I have only been able to deliver half my load for the past two years. Because of my flaw you have to do all this work and you don't get full value for your efforts.' The water bearer felt sorry for the cracked pot, and said compassionately, 'As we return to my master's house I want you to notice the beautiful flowers growing along the path.'

"And, as they went up the hill the cracked pot saw the sun warming the beautiful wild flowers on one side of the path. But at the end of the path the cracked pot felt bad once again because it had leaked out half its contents, and so again it apologized to the water bearer for its failure.

"The water bearer said to the pot: 'Did you notice there were flowers only on your side of the path? Not on the other side. That's because I have always known about your flaw, so I took advantage of it. I planted flower seeds on your side of the path, and every day when we walked back from the stream you've watered them. For the past two years I've been able to pick beautiful flowers for my master's table. Without you being just the way you are, I would not have had these beautiful flowers to grace my master's table.'"

I could tell where Jesus was going with this story. "So the pot, although flawed, was of some use to the water bearer," I responded.

"Right!" Jesus said. "Everyone has their own unique flaws. Nobody is perfect. You are all cracked pots. But my Father in Heaven will use those flaws to the further glory of His Name, somehow. In God's great plan…nothing goes to waste."

It always amazed me how much I still had to learn from Jesus.

INTERLUDE:

I was sitting with Jesus on the porch one morning, not really talking, not really doing anything much, just thinking. I was thinking about faith. Why, I wondered, is faith easier for some people but then so hard for others? I talk to a lot of people who tell me they're just incapable of faith, the kind of faith necessary to believe the Bible and accept the saving grace of God through Jesus Christ. They say it's all so much fantasy to them, like a fairytale, or believing in the Tooth Fairy. I find that I have trouble with faith too, sometimes. Perhaps I'm too intellectual, too much a person of the American school system to believe in something that does not use the scientific method of logical deduction. Then again, maybe I'm just too inundated with the ways of the world.

I started mentioning this to Jesus as we sat on the porch. I didn't think he'd have much to say about it, but he did.

"You know Rob, I've often wondered the same thing," he said sadly. "I had the same mix of people among my disciples: some found it easy to believe, others had a hard time of it. Peter seemed to have faith, at least he was the most vocal about having it, but oft times he disappointed me with his lack of faith."

"Yes, I know," I agreed. "The cock crowing at dawn and all that."

"Precisely," he said. "Others of my disciples had lots of faith, and it came to them naturally. Mary and Martha for example. It seems to me that some people are naturally inclined to have faith."

"While others have to work very hard for even a little faith," I added.

"Yes, unfortunately. I would try to help them, but sometimes they have to work it out for themselves, with the help of the Holy Spirit."

"I wish there were a way for us to help them with their faith," I lamented.

"Well," Jesus said, "they could always look back at the ones who never gave up their faith, even under terrible duress and the threat of death."

"Like the apostles?"

"Right," Jesus said.

Just so. There were many among the disciples who held to their faith in Jesus even when threatened with death. This gave me an idea. I got my laptop and started doing some digging. In a little while I had some useful information.

"Okay, I've come up with some interesting historical facts," I told Jesus. "Of the 12 Apostles you had back then, 11 of them died horribly, 12 if you include Judas as the 13th."

Jesus didn't respond to that, he just sat listening, a look of extreme sorrow on his face that I hated to see. I continued.

"Peter (or Simon before you renamed him), the one who had such a hard time with his faith? He was crucified like you, but because he didn't want to die exactly as you did; he requested they nail him to the cross upside down. So they did. But he never lost his faith. He had become strong in faith after your resurrection."

"My dear Peter, the rock..." Jesus said softly.

"Paul," I continued, "who was Saul before his conversion on the Damascus Road, was beheaded by sword under Nero. Since he was technically a Roman citizen he couldn't be crucified. He stayed true to you to the very end.

"Andrew was crucified on an X-shaped cross, praising you to the end. Thomas, the twin, went to India. At one city he was ordered by the king to be led out and stabbed with spears by four soldiers. He never renounced you. Matthew, as well as Matthias (the one they picked to replace Judas) were stoned and burned, yet never wavered in their faith. James, one of the sons of Zeebedee, was put to death by sword at the order of King Herod. And Bartholomew, who was called Nathaniel in the Gospel of John, had the worst death of all! They nailed him to a post and flayed him alive; then, when he wasn't dead yet they beheaded him. He could have saved himself at any time during all that if he had renounced you. But he didn't."

When I looked up Jesus' head was down. I believe he was weeping slightly. "I knew about all that," he whispered. "I wish I didn't know, but I do. I wish there were a better way, but my Father had other plans. And I think you've discovered part of His plan: to have these saints serve as inspiration for the generations to come, so they could look back and see how those who had faith held on to it tenaciously even unto death. Greater love hath no man."

I could feel Jesus' sadness at being reminded of the deaths of his friends and followers, but the fact that so many believers back then went to their deaths—and some very terrible deaths—without losing their faith in Jesus was just amazing to me. I mean, the apostles were not supermen. They were basically ignorant cowards at the start of Jesus' mission. And dense. They never seemed to get the depth of what Jesus was saying. And after Jesus was crucified they ran and cowered in a dark room, hiding from the authorities, afraid they would be next. But it was this group of slackers, these uneducated "fraidy-cats" that, after the resurrection, became emboldened by the Holy Spirit of God and preached the Gospel unafraid of the consequences. They became fearless promoters of Christianity, and never lost their faith after that, even if it meant torture and a horrible death. Something must have happened to those men to make them into what they became. They certainly didn't start that way. But somehow they found the faith to become courageous evangelists in Jesus' name. They believed in Jesus and his resurrection with all their hearts and souls. It's hard to imagine someone would go to their death for a false faith, let alone so many.

And there was more. Luke, the author of the third Gospel and of Acts, was hanged in Greece after preaching about Jesus. James the Just, brother of Jesus and the leader of the church in Jerusalem, was thrown down the stairs at the southeast wall of the Temple, over a hundred feet, but didn't die right away. Nor did he deny his faith. When his enemies saw he had survived the fall, they beat him to death with clubs. Jesus' youngest brother, Jude, was shot with arrows when he refused to renounce his belief in Christ. Only one apostle survived to die in old age: John, the other brother of Zebedee. He was threatened with boiling in oil, but miraculously escaped. He was later sentenced to the mines on the prison island of Patmos, where he wrote the Book of Revelation. His faith was strong to the end.

"You know," I said to Jesus, "I'm not sure my faith would be as strong as the apostles' if I was threatened with death. I think I would cave-in, unlike your disciples."

"Fortunately you don't have to," Jesus said. "These days hardly anyone is going to threaten you with death for your faith, at least in this country. But there are other places were things aren't so free, and people die for me all the time. But you, Rob, would hardly ever find yourself in a similar position."

This was very true. In this country religious freedom is fundamental; it's part of our governing philosophy. No one will threaten me about my religion, or demand I renounce Christ or die. Not so in other third-world countries I've heard, but here in America, the only pressure you have to lose your faith is peer pressure.

"That's true, I guess," I said. "But I really don't think my faith would be strong enough to hold out if I was threatened with death. I know I'm basically a coward about dying, and if someone were to tell me to either renounce my faith or die...I seriously think I would give in and renounce you. Of course it would be a lie, but I think I would lie to save my own life." I was not proud of this admission, but I believed it was a true assessment of my character.

I saw Jesus smile slightly, and I was amazed at how happy it made me to see him smile. "Well Rob," he said, "you are fortunate indeed that you will probably never have to go through such an experience. But, should the worst ever happen, and someone says to you that you have to renounce me or they will kill you...to tell you the truth, I'd rather that you lie about it and tell them that you renounce me."

This surprised me. "Really?" I said. "You'd rather I renounce you and the Christian religion rather than die a martyr to the faith?"

"The time of martyrs is over," Jesus said to me. "As I said, my Father in Heaven has a plan, and part of that plan was to have faithful believers in the past for people today to look back on as a source of inspiration in their faith, believers who stayed true to the faith and preached my death and resurrection without fear, in the face of great danger. But that was at the start. They served their purpose. The Christian faith is much stronger today; we don't really need people to die for the faith, at least most of the time. I believe in life, and I want you and everyone to live their lives to the fullest. I don't want anyone to die before their time. Not even for me or the Christian faith.

Renounce me today so I can forgive you tomorrow, and live to pray another day. Remember, I'm all about forgiveness. I will forgive you your lapse of faith if you repent of it and come back to me. But do try to save your life if you have to."

"That's awfully understanding of you Jesus."

"Hey," Jesus replied, "if I don't understand you people, who does?"

"That's another big Amen!" I said.

Chapter Twelve: The Tolerant One

One Saturday morning a friend from church drove up to the side of my house and approached the porch while I sat there with Jesus. She had a wad of papers in her hand. When I saw it was Dorothy I knew what to expect. She was probably coming to ask me to sign another petition. She was always circulating petitions around the neighborhood and at church for one cause or another. Apparently she was extremely liberal.

"Good morning Dorothy," I called to her as she came up to the porch. "Looks like you have another petition."

"How d'ya guess?" she asked sarcastically as she came up to the porch huffing and puffing from the effort of crossing the lawn. She thrust the papers she was holding toward me, and I took them before they could smash into my face.

"So what's this one," I asked as I glanced at the lengthy petition she had formally drafted with her impeccable precision. To my horror I saw, after a cursory glance at the draft, that it had something to do with "same-sex" marriage. Oh no…

Jesus was sitting in his rocker, as usual, but of course Dorothy didn't know that. He must have seen the concerned look on my face. "What's wrong?" he asked. "What is it?"

I sort of ignored the question, since I didn't want to start talking to Jesus while Dorothy was there. Although I was sure she'd understand my having a chair for Jesus and all, I never felt comfortable telling her about it.

"Hmm," I hummed as I scanned the pages Dorothy had handed me. "Well Dorothy, would it be okay if I thought about this one for a while before I signed it?" I was stalling for time.

Dorothy gave me a harsh look. "Well, okay, but don't take too long. I have to get as many signatures as I can to our Congressman by the end of the month."

"I just want to talk it over with Lucy is all," I said. I was giving Jesus "the eye" as I said that, and I think Dorothy noticed, because the look on her face became more severe.

"Don't tell me you're one of <u>those</u> people," she demanded.

Boy, did I hate being one of <u>those</u> people, whoever <u>they</u> were. "What do you mean?"

She glared at me. "People who are prejudice toward our homosexual brothers and sisters of course," she said. "You're not one of those are you? You believe gays ought to have the right to get married if they want to, don't you?"

"Well, I…"

"Robert!" she said. Oh how I hate it when people call me Robert: it makes me nervous. Only my wife when she's angry with me and traffic police call me Robert (it's the name that appears on my license). "I always thought you had an open mind. Don't you think gays should have the same rights under the law as other people?"

"I'm not sure I understand the issues involved Dorothy," I pleaded with her. You did <u>not</u> want to get on Dorothy's bad side. "I mean, what 'rights' are we talking about?"

"For one," she snapped, "the right to have your spouse inherit your estate. Or to be covered by medical and life insurance, or be a beneficiary. Unless they can get legally married, gay people don't have those rights. Didn't you know that?"

She was obviously becoming a bit disgruntled with me. I thought about it for a second. "Seems to me it would be easier to change the insurance and inheritance laws than to change the marriage laws?"

This didn't sit well with Dorothy. "That's not all," she exclaimed. "There are all sorts of things that negatively affect these people because they can't get legally married: social security, spousal tax dependency, legal wills, estate management, investments…it's a long list of privileges that are being withheld from these citizens."

Dorothy obviously believed strongly in what she was endorsing. But I was not that sure. Seemed most of these "issues" were monetary: people concerned they were not going to get the money they believed they deserved. "Please Dorothy," I asked. "Just let me talk it over with my wife, think on it a little bit, and I'll get back to you as soon as I can." Even as I said that last statement I knew it probably wasn't true; I wouldn't get back to her because I didn't want to sign her petition. I didn't believe in the cause. To me, homosexuality was a sin, forbidden by God. I did not want to go on record as advocating it. I was hoping that in a few days Dorothy would forget she asked me about it. I could only hope.

Dorothy wasn't buying my appeal. She seemed to be trying to determine if I was sincere or not. Finally she said: "Well, okay. I'll see you at church tomorrow. You can sign it then, okay?"

"Do you really want to bring a petition like that to church?" I asked. It just didn't seem appropriate to me.

"Why?" she asked earnestly. "What's wrong with it?"

I didn't want to get into this discussion with Dorothy <u>right</u> <u>then</u>. "Oh, nothing I guess. See you tomorrow." She nodded with a grunt, turned to her car and was gone before I could stop holding my breath.

When she had gone Jesus looked at me with an accusatory expression. "You ignored me."

"Sorry," I apologized. "I just never felt comfortable around Dorothy. She's always going on about one cause or another. A lot of crazy free-thinking stuff most of the time. She makes me nervous."

"I don't see why you have to be nervous around her," Jesus opined. "She seems like a nice enough lady to me."

"That's because you don't know her," I replied. Then I realized who I was talking to, and cringed inwardly. "She's just a bit flighty."

"I think I can guess what that petition she wanted you to sign is about."

I wasn't sure I wanted to address this topic with Jesus at the present moment. Then I decided it might be best to get it out in the open. "She wants to petition the state to allow same-sex marriages," I said.

"Ah yes, that one," Jesus said, nodding knowingly.

I was surprised Jesus seemed informed on the topic, although I shouldn't have been. So now I had an opportunity to ask Jesus a really loaded question. "What do you think about same-sex marriages?"

Jesus smiled that incredible smile of his. "I was wondering when you get to that question."

Okay…so far so good. I decided to be more direct. "So would <u>you</u> sign the petition? How do you feel about the subject?"

"Are you asking me personally or are you asking the God part of me?"

"There's a difference?"

"Good response," he said. Then, after a short pause: "I agree with you, Rob. It does seem easier to change the insurance laws and all the assorted smaller laws that are causing the issues she was talking about rather than changing the state marriage law."

While I was pleased Jesus agreed with me on that point, I had a sense he was evading the real question. "But that's the legal point of view. What's your religious take on the issue?"

Jesus sighed and looked straight into my eyes. "It's — a — sin," he said slowly and purposely.

"That's all?" I couldn't believe that was all he had to say on the matter. "I know it's a sin, but where do you stand on the whole homosexual issue in general?"

He was looking at me as a parent might look at a child who just didn't understand. "Rob, it's a sin: an affront to my Father in Heaven. It needs repentance and forgiveness. But in that sense it is not unlike other sins, such as adultery. One sin is not worse than the other, not in the eyes of my Father. Adultery and fornication are sins.   So is homosexuality. They're all sins, in need of forgiving. To hate one sin more than the other is not consistent. That would <u>not</u> be real justice, and my Father is <u>passionate</u> about justice. Why would He condemn one sinner more than the other?"

I was trying to absorb what Jesus had just said. I wasn't sure if he was saying he disapproved of same-sex marriage or not? "I'm not sure what you're saying," I admitted. "Are you saying we should <u>not</u> legalize same-sex marriage?"

"Rob, 'holy matrimony,' if that's what you're talking about, the binding of two souls together as one, is a private matter between the individuals and my Father. But I think you're talking about the legal institution of marriage in your culture, and that is purely a matter between the couple and the governing state; it's secular, not spiritual. I don't comment on your legal system. You know that."

"Okay," I quickly back-peddled, "what I meant was…spiritually, should we allow sinners such as these to enter into the state of holy matrimony?" I thought I clarified that pretty well.

"Sinners? You mean those who commit the sin of homosexuality?" he asked.

"Yes, that's what I'm asking about."

"Well Rob, as I was just explaining to you, I and my Father do not see the difference between two adulterers and two homosexuals. Both couples are committing sin."

"Ah, okay..." I said, trying to zero-in on the point. "So, should we allow church ministers, for example, to perform marriage ceremonies for homosexual couples?"

"Rob, you're not listening. Think about it. You folks today don't seem to have a problem performing the marriage ceremony for heterosexual couples who are living in sin."

"Huh?" Now I was confused.

"Come on Rob, do I have to remind you of what you probably already know? Isn't it true that some Christian ministers, even after finding out the couple they're about to marry has been living with each other for months—sometimes years—still perform the marriage ceremony for the couple before the eyes of God, their family and everyone present? It doesn't seem to bother those in attendance, or the minister of God, that the two are actively engaging in sin with no show of remorse or repentance."

Okay... I really hadn't thought of that. He was right, though. Slowly over the decades fewer priests, pastors and Christian ministers were objecting to the obvious hypocrisy of marrying couples who were already having sex. Maybe in previous generations couples tried to hide this fact from the preacher if it was true, but not anymore. Not much at least. Often the couple is publically living together, with the full knowledge of the family and the minister performing the ceremony, but objections to this are very rare these days. I think Jesus' point was: how does marrying a homosexual couple differ from marrying a heterosexual couple who are also engaging in sin openly? I wasn't sure I had an answer for that.

"Perhaps the difficulty," I guessed, "is that the heterosexual couple's sin is mitigated after they marry; coming together as husband and wife legitimatizes what would otherwise be considered adultery. Of course any past sin is still there and needs repentance, but once they're married there is no adultery. But does it work that way in a gay marriage? Is there no sin if they're married?"

"Rob, as always you've managed to distill the problem to the root," Jesus said. "But you're asking about <u>allowing</u> gay couples to marry, which again is a legal question, and one I will not comment on. But I see no difference in 'allowing' heterosexual couples to marry. They too may still be sinning; that's a matter between them and the Lord. Sinners sin; all we can do is encourage people not to sin. But you don't have to beat them up about it or be prejudicial toward them."

"And that's what I'm talking about Jesus," I said. "Tolerance. Aren't we, as Christians, supposed to be tolerant? Aren't we supposed to tolerate differing points of view and perspectives?"

"Well, yes," Jesus said. "Tolerance is good, but it can only go so far. Nowadays the only thing that's not tolerated is <u>intolerance</u>."

"You know, you're right!" I agreed immediately. "If we live up to our principles, and preach the Bible, we're called intolerant, and that's a big cultural taboo these days. So how can we preach the Bible in a world that puts such a high value on tolerance?"

"Does your world value tolerance more than truth?" Jesus asked.

"No, of course not," I hurriedly countered, although I was not sure I was right. "But we have to change with the times, and this is a direction a lot of people want the church to change. So, as your <u>church</u>," I pointed my finger at Jesus, "can we, or should we, be tolerant?"

Jesus stared at my finger until I became self-conscious and dropped my hand. "It's <u>your</u> church too," he said softly.

That diffused me. I calmed down immediately. "Okay, <u>our</u> church. Should we be tolerant?"

"This question," he began, "is much more complicated than you think."

"How so?" I asked.

"It has many facets; the legal side for one. Should my followers legally tolerate other views, other religions with different perspectives? Yes! We should all defend the legal rights of everyone, no matter what religion or creed they belong to. You may not agree with their beliefs, but you <u>must</u> tolerate them. I don't want my followers imposing their beliefs on others. Remember, it's supposed to be about love. To love me you must have a change of heart. I <u>propose</u> this to everyone; I don't <u>impose</u> it on anyone."

"Kind of like attracting them rather than attacking them," I said, secretly pleased with my word play.

"Nice one," Jesus said as he winked at me. "But there's more. For example, should you be socially tolerant of other religious views in the community? Or more to the point, if you have a sister or brother, or a colleague or neighbor that disagrees with you on religious grounds, should you tolerate them?"

"My guess," I answered, "would be yes."

"And you would be right, Rob."

"Well that just sounds like loving your neighbor."

"There ya go!" Jesus laughed, slapping me on the back. I have to admit, I just <u>love</u> those slaps on the back from Jesus. "Always love your neighbor. I didn't say you had to <u>agree</u> with them. No, even if you disagree with them you must love and serve them just as you do for your Christian brothers and sisters."

"Even if they're Muslim or Buddhist?" I asked.

"Unquestionably," Jesus replied. "But at the same time you have a wonderful opportunity to share your beliefs and tell them about me and about the saving grace of my Father. These are the ones you <u>should</u> be talking to about me. And if they choose not to believe you, to not believe in me, don't just write them off as if they're lost causes. No! You must still love them and serve them, all the while with the hope that their hearts will change and they will one day turn toward me."

"Now hold on," I said. I thought I had caught Jesus in an inconsistency. "I seem to remember in the Bible you told your disciples: 'If anyone will not welcome you or listen to your words, leave that home or town and shake the dust off your feet (Matt 10:14).' Are you telling me now that you were wrong? Didn't you tell them to write off those who wouldn't listen to them?"

"Rob, that was the first time I was sending the disciples out to preach the Good News," Jesus said. "It was a trial run, and I didn't want them wasting their time. I knew they would come across people who would listen to them and some who would not listen. Sometimes a strong-willed leader might convince a whole town not to believe my disciples, and I didn't want them to lose time trying to convince those people. I wanted to see how affective they would be, so I gave them those instructions to make sure they covered as much territory at first as they could. Nowadays you have the time to spend on the stubborn ones. Often they're the only ones left after you've convinced the more open-minded ones. But back then we didn't have the time to spend convincing the doubters. I wanted them to spread the Good News to as many interested people as possible."

Okay, I could buy that. So far I was following everything Jesus said. But now I thought it was time to ask him the big question. "Okay, I can see all that. But should we theologically tolerate other points of view inside the church?" I knew this was a tough question.

"What do you mean?" Jesus asked.

I was thinking frantically. "For example, there are a few people at my church who believe in the rapture, and some who don't. Some of us sometimes speak in tongues, but most of us don't." I was running out of examples. "Some think infant baptism is wrong, that we should wait until the age of consent... There are lots of other issues like that running all through most Christian churches."

"Rob, those are secondary issues that most communities have, and your community needs to tolerate them. You can talk about them, discuss the differences and debate the issues if you like, but don't fight about them. These are not dividing issues, just relative topics. They don't endanger your salvation."

I knew better than to ask Jesus which side of those issues he stood on. We had a kind of silent understanding that I would never put him on the spot like that. And I agreed with him on this as well. "Like the differences between brothers and sisters in the same family," I said. "You know, they're just scraps, not shootouts."

"On the nose!" Jesus said, poking his nose with his index finger as in Charades.

"And we shouldn't argue over differences," I restated.

"Not if it keeps you from the more important things," Jesus said. "Do you remember when I said to the Pharisees: 'You blind guides! You strain out a gnat but swallow a camel!' (Matt 23:24)? I was scolding them for being too concerned with themselves and not practicing mercy, charity and forgiveness."

"So we shouldn't waste time worrying about those kinds of differences," I said.

Jesus held up a finger, the gesture he used when he was making a special point. "Ah, but there are differences," he said, "and then there are <u>distinctions</u>. Some things <u>define</u> my disciples from others; the beliefs that describe who and what they are, such as: there is one God in three persons. That's not a difference, that's part of the definition of a Christian. I am God's Son, who lived and died on the cross in your place, and rose as your savior. That's not a difference, that's an <u>assertion</u>. The Bible is the Word of God. That's a defining statement too. These are basic definitions of who you are."

"So those differences are the <u>big</u> differences?"

"Yes," he said. "Tolerating differences here would be to lose your identity as a Christian. But there are other differences, the ones that differentiate the various denominations within Christianity, that are more or less cultural differences than anything else, and these delineate the various churches that exist today. But these differences, although many make much of them, are not as momentous as you might think."

"You mean you feel the differences in the denominations are not that important?" I asked.

"Oh, they're important to <u>you people</u>," he said. "The separation into Catholic, Baptist, Lutheran, Presbyterian, Methodist, Reformed, Pentecostal... <u>et cetera</u>. Most of the differences are legalistic, and only serve to further define the intricacies of Christianity and salvation. A lot of the differences are just commentary on the major points, like repentance and forgiveness, but do not significantly affect your salvation. Some others are just a matter of style. So no, I don't make much of a fuss over these differences."

"You don't believe in the separation of denominations?" I asked.

"Oh, I <u>believe</u> in them," he said. "How could I not? Every time I turn around you people are establishing another denomination. It's a little hard to follow sometimes, but I understand why there are these differences. Humans are quite complex and varied. And the feeling is that my Father is too big to be explained by one ideology. But just like your separate states in America get along, even though they're different and distinct from each other, they're still the United States."

"So you're saying having a preference for one Christian denomination over another is comparable to preferring one state over the other? Say, Texas over Nebraska?"

"Yeah, something like that," Jesus said. "While you might recognize the differences, each one has its own unique quality. But, in keeping with your metaphor Rob, as long as you don't cross a 'national boundary,' you should still be okay."

I had one final question on this topic. "What about moral and ethical differences? Should we tolerate those kinds of differences?"

"Are you talking about my followers or non-Christians?" he asked.

"Your followers," I said. "Christians in general."

"Good!" he said. "Because the main enemy of Christianity is <u>not</u> non-Christians…it's bad Christianity, or rather, those who say they follow me but live as the unbelievers do. It sends the wrong message. My followers should reflect me; they should exhibit love and compassion. And I want my followers to be forgiving. It all centers on forgiveness. No matter who you are, no matter what you've done, you can come to me. Just as you are. But it doesn't stop there. Oh no! I will change your heart. You will not stay the way you are. You can't, and still be my follower. I am open to everyone and anyone, but it's not <u>anyone</u> who, in the end, becomes my disciple. My love will change you, so if you want to remain the way you are—the sinner you are—don't look to me, because I will make you into a new person, with a new heart. And the grace of my Father will smooth out all the differences, in the end."

What else could I add to that?

Chapter Thirteen: The Scary Ones

It was Halloween, and I loved Halloween. I know there are some Christians who do not like Halloween, being full of pagan images as well as scarier things like ghosts and devils and witches, etc. But I loved Halloween, and so did my wife. When I was a kid I always had a lot of fun at Halloween, trick-or-treating with my friends, dressing up…it was a lot of fun. And as I got older it continued to be fun. The Halloween parties I attended as a young adult were always the best parties of the year. I don't know… there's something about dressing up in crazy costumes that makes people act a lot different from their usual personalities. Halloween was always about fun for me.

A while back there were some folks at my church who tried to get a movement going to ban Halloween in our town, or at least ban celebrating it at the church, but it never caught on with the congregation. But I still knew of people who vehemently objected to Christians celebrating or even recognizing Halloween. I always thought it was harmless fun. But then I had to reconsider after talking to a few of the more vocal objectors last Halloween. They had pointed out that Halloween was a pagan holiday, from the ancient Celtic festival of <u>Samhain</u>, usually observed November 1st. The ancient Celts would light bonfires and wear crazy costumes to fend off wayward spirits. Not to mention the habit our culture had of dressing our children up in costumes that depicted Satan, the enemy of God, and witches, Satan's minions. All of this was sinful they had said. I reluctantly had to agree with them. What they said seemed right.

I was all ready to take down my Halloween decorations last year when I spoke to our pastor. He said that it was all right to celebrate Halloween. The pope back in the ninth century designated November 1st as a time to honor all saints and martyrs, so <u>that</u> holiday—All Saints' Day—was the one Christians were celebrating. The church back then incorporated some of the traditions of Samhain into the celebration, that's all. So I put the Halloween decorations back up.

That was last year. This year I had a little pro-active conversation with a deacon friend of mine from church about Halloween, just in case anyone said anything to me about celebrating Halloween. I told him what the pastor had said about All Saint's Day. He pointed out that the day before traditionally has been known as "All Hallows' Eve," which later became "Halloween." Over the course of centuries it evolved into a secular, community-based event characterized by child-friendly activities such as trick-or-treating. I felt okay again about celebrating Halloween.

So there I was, putting up the webbing and the ghosties and ghoulies and long-legged beasties and things that go bump in the night, and I was feeling pretty pleased with myself. It was October 31st, and I was getting ready for trick-or-treaters. When I finished with the decorations I got my coffee and sat in my chair on the porch. Jesus was there of course, sitting quietly, looking at the people going by on the street. But for some reason I felt guilty. I mean, there I was sitting with Jesus on the porch, and we were getting ready to celebrate what amounted to a pagan holiday by dressing children up in costumes of the devil, witches and ghosts, all symbols of death and wickedness. I just couldn't reconcile these thoughts in my mind with my Christianity.

"You seem uncomfortable about something, Rob," Jesus commented. He was always very intuitive about my feelings.

"Yes, I am," I admitted. "It's all this Halloween stuff we put up every year, and the celebration of Halloween in general."

"Let me guess," Jesus said. "You're upset because you're celebrating a pagan holiday, right?"

I nodded guiltily.

"Well, don't feel guilty," he said. "It's more of a cultural thing than a religious thing. Maybe back hundreds of years ago it meant something to the pagans of old Ireland and Europe, but today it's largely just a cultural remnant."

"But aren't you upset over the way Christians embrace the old pagan myths? Doesn't it upset you to see how we dress our children in unchristian costumes representing mythological entities that are still profane figures? There are a lot of Christians today who say we shouldn't be celebrating Halloween at all."

"Well, they're just spoiled sports," Jesus said.

"Come again?" I wasn't sure I heard him correctly.

"I said they're just spoiled sports," Jesus repeated.

"Spoiled sports? You don't think we're committing a sin by celebrating Halloween and dressing up the kids in all those horrific outfits?"

"Well, if you people attached any real meaning to all those things, then yes, I'd be upset. But you don't. At least most of you don't. As far as I can see, you're just having fun."

"And you don't object to our having fun with old pagan superstitions?" I asked.

"Hey, you're only human," Jesus said with a smile. "I think the celebration at this time of year was a reflection of your ancestor's collective apprehension of the coming winter. Everything dies in winter, the harvest is over, the days are getting shorter and the nights are getting longer and colder. I'm sure your ancestors needed some kind of release from the tension of the coming darkness, and traditionally all through the world people have been ushering in winter with gatherings, costumes, feasting and sweets. I would never object to harmless celebration to release tension."

I was surprised by his attitude. "So you don't mind all the celebration associated with evil?" I asked.

"Evil?" Jesus exclaimed. "You think it's about evil? After all we've said about evil? No, this celebration you call Halloween isn't about anything evil, it's about fear and ignorance, at least that's how it all started."

"Fear and ignorance?" I echoed.

"Rob, the end of October and the beginning of November marked the end of summer and beginning of the dark, cold winter. This was a time your ancestors associated with death, and rightly so. They would build huge bonfires and wear costumes with the heads and skins of animals to try to keep the spirits away. Then, when the celebration was over they would relight their own hearth fires in their homes, which they had put out for the celebration, with flames from the sacred bonfire, to keep them safe during the coming winter. Your ancestors were afraid of the winter, and because they were ignorant about what controlled things like the sun and the wind; they did what they could to stave off the fear of death intrinsic to the coming winter season."

"So they were afraid, that's why they came up with the celebration?"

"Exactly!" Jesus said. "And I would never tell them they couldn't continue with the tradition, for that's all it is: a cultural tradition. Of course you folks know all about the weather and such things these days, so you're not petitioning any deity for the sun to come back or anything like that. You're just going through the motions, similar to what your ancestors did centuries ago. Your culture traditionally does a lot of stuff that's just a reflection of the old days."

"We do?" I asked.

"Sure," he responded. "For instance, most people got married in June way back when because that's when they took their yearly bath, May or June. But just in case they still smelled badly the brides carried a bouquet of flowers to disguise the body odor. You folks still hold to that tradition today, even though most of your brides bathe regularly and smell really nice. It's just a tradition. There's no meaning in it."

"And you don't mind that our celebration of Halloween includes all those pagan trappings?" I asked.

"Mind?" Jesus said. "Why should I mind? You do the same thing with Easter and Christmas."

Now I knew about the pagan embellishments associated with our holidays of Easter and Christmas. There were certainly no eggs or bunny rabbits running around in the resurrection story of Jesus in the Bible. Likewise there were no Christmas trees or pretty lights or Yule logs when Jesus was born. But our celebration of these holidays includes many of the trappings of old pagan rituals.

"Yes, I know we use a lot of pagan traditions in our celebration of Christmas and Easter," I admitted to Jesus.

"More so than Halloween, really," Jesus added. "The very name 'Easter' comes from the old Anglo-Saxon goddess of fertility <u>Eastra</u>. That the same goddess as Ishtar and Astarte or "Ashtoreth" in the Old Testament. There used to be a great spring festival held in her honor in the old days. She was a fertility goddess and she was symbolized by an egg and the reproductively fruitful March hare, or rabbit. The tradition you folks have of coloring and exchanging eggs comes from when your ancestors used to dye them in spring colors and give them to friends and family as gifts. It wasn't until the year 190 AD that Pope Victor I declared officially that the festival of my resurrection would be celebrated at the same time of year as the old Easter celebration. And that's when people began to mix up the names of the festivals. After centuries it evolved into the celebration you have today. But Easter is just a name, an old name that you folks have held onto from ancient times. It's just a tradition. I seriously doubt anyone knows where the term came from anymore."

"And it's the same for Christmas, right?" I said.

"Yes, it is," Jesus agreed. "The Roman festival of Saturnalia at the end of the year was very popular back then, and many of the accouterments associated with that celebration, as well as the 'Yule Tide' traditions from northern Europe and the Norse culture, were incorporated into the Christmas celebration. I'm sure you realize there were no Christmas trees in Judea when I was born."

"Yes, I realize that," I said. "And December 25th is not really your birthday, is it?"

Jesus' face reddened slightly. Did I embarrass him? "Well, no, it's not. I guess that's widely known these days," he admitted.

"Seems I remember my friend Johnny telling me that Mithras and Horus and other old-world deities were said to be born on December 25th because that was the day the ancients thought the sun started coming back up in the sky and the days started to get longer again."

"Very good Rob," Jesus said. "That's right. December 25th was the traditional day to celebrate the end of the year and beginning of the new one. It was a time to look to new beginnings. It was quite a party. And the people didn't want to lose that party atmosphere at the end of the year, so a lot of the trimmings and embellishments that went with that pagan celebration got incorporated into the Christian Christmas celebration. In the 17th century the partying got a bit out-of-hand, and in some areas they decided to ban the celebration of Christmas. The Holy Day remained, they still recognized my birth, but they didn't allow any celebration in the traditional sense. This didn't go over very well with the populace, as I'm sure you suspected."

"Yeah, they didn't keep Christmas illegal for very long," I said.

"No, they didn't. People get used to things, and they get very upset when you start changing things up."

"You don't have to tell me that," I agreed. "But tell me... When is your real birthday?"

Jesus smiled. "Now you know they didn't pay all that much attention to birthdays back in my time, don't you? Actually only astrologers and those interested in magic and such kept track of birth dates. To the Jews celebrating the birth of a child was prideful, an excuse to party and indulge in drinking, so they tended to frown on it."

"But surely you knew what day of the year you were born on?"

"Yes, I knew, but that was just family information; it wasn't written down in the family Torah or anything like that." Jesus winked. "We just used birth dates for specific milestones, like coming-of-age, or things like that. We didn't celebrate our birthday every year as you folks do. So yeah, I knew when I was born, but we didn't talk about it so much, and we didn't make such a fuss over it."

"So what day of the year was it really?" I knew I was pressing the question, but I just had to ask.

"I'm not really sure anymore, to tell you the truth," Jesus said, winking again and nicely evading the question. "I seem to remember it was in the spring. Close to Passover. But the date is not important."

"I know," I assured him," I was just curious."

"Why? Are you thinking of throwing me a party?"

"No, nothing like that," I said. "That's still at Christmas." Seems I wasn't going to find out the exact date of Jesus' birth. I think he was trying to tell me he would rather I focus on more important things, like love and forgiveness. "But getting back to the point...I'm glad our using those old traditions and customs from old pagan religions doesn't bother you too much, but I still feel guilty over some of the traditions we still observe for Halloween."

"You folks use all sorts of old pagan traditions in your everyday life. If you want to feel guilty about something, why not feel guilty over the names of the days of the week?"

"Names of the days of the week?" I did not understand the reference Jesus was making.

"Yeah, the names for the days of the week. You know: Monday, Tuesday…those?"

"What about them?" I asked.

"Rob, didn't you know that the days of the week are named after pagan deities? Just like the names of the planets?"

"They are?"

"Yes!" Jesus said. "Sunday is named after…well, you know: the sun. And I'll bet you can guess some of the rest."

I thought about it for a moment. "Sure, I guess so. That would mean Monday is named after the moon?"

"Right! The ancient Greeks called it '<u>hemera selenes</u>' or 'day of the moon.' And Tuesday is named for the Norse god Týr. Wednesday is the Norse god Odin's day, or 'Woden' as he was also called, and Thursday's…"

"Wait!" I thought I could guess that one. "It's named after Odin's son Thor, right?"

"Correct," Jesus said. "Friday is named after Odin's wife Frigga. Saturday is easy to guess…"

"The Roman god Saturn, right?"

"Right," Jesus confirmed.

I had never thought about the reasons for the names of the week. I guess I took them for granted, just as everyone else does. "So the days of the week are named after pagan gods," I mused. "I never knew that. But that doesn't bother you?"

"Bother me? No," Jesus said. "My Father only named one of the days of the week, the first day, the day He rested. He called it the 'Sabbath' day. The other days were more or less left up to you people to name if you wanted to. Originally we just used numbers, you know, the second day of the week, the third, and so on."

"But the fact that our ancestors used pagan deities for the names of the week doesn't bother you?"

"No, why should it? You people do the same thing with some of the name of the months too. January is named for the Roman god Janus, the so called 'god of beginnings.' February is named after <u>Februa</u>, the Roman word for 'smoke'; it was the month they held their festival of purification. March is named after the Roman god of war: Mars. April comes from the Latin <u>Aprilis</u>, which was a time of fertility (it was believed this was the month when the earth opened for the plants to grow). May comes from Maia, a Roman goddess of growth and increase. And June..."

I thought I could guess this one. "Wait, I think I know: Juno right? The wife of Zeus?"

"Wrong!" Jesus said. "Zeus is Greek. <u>Juno</u> was the wife of Jupiter, the Roman equivalent of Zeus."

"Oh, right," I said. I knew that for cryin' out loud. I just wasn't thinking. But I had no idea pagan mythologies was so prevalent in the things we use every day but take for granted. "I really didn't know any of that Jesus," I admitted. "Seems we use words and phrases and other stuff from pagan mythology all the time, we just don't think about it."

"That's okay," Jesus said. "Don't go feeling guilty over imagined slights you might have committed. Your traditions, customs and rituals from bygone eras are merely remembrances of days long gone. The names of the week were incorporated by your ancestors as far back as the third century. This was because the Christian church was starting to absorb a lot of pagan cultures, and this in turn caused a lot of people to become interested in these cultures, and in things like astrology. This speculation caused them to start using the planetary names for the weeks, because as you might have noticed, the seven days of the week correspond to the seven objects in the sky that move against the stars and can be seen by the unaided eye."

Yet another fact I was unaware of. "Boy Jesus, you sure do make me feel uninformed sometimes."

"Well, I've had a lot of time to study up," he said.

Chapter Fourteen: The Readers

I love bookstores. Although they're a dying breed these days, I still love bookstores. Just show me a Border's or a Barnes & Noble store and I'll spend the whole day just perusing the shelves. So the other day when I was in town going to the bank and the post office I decided to drop in on a favorite of mine: a tiny, privately owned bookstore called the Regal Reading Room. I knew the owner, Cathy, because I was a frequently visitor, and we often chatted about books and things whenever I came by.

Since Christmas was coming I wanted to look for a spiritual book as a gift for my wife. She loved reading inspirational literature, and this little bookstore was a good source for such material. I waved to Cathy as I strolled in to the store, and I immediately went to the back, to the Religious Books section.

As I was scanning the titles on the "Christian" shelves I noticed the other sections filled with New Age books and various other spiritual and religious material: Eastern Mysticism, Buddhism, Taoism, Bahá'í, Gnosticism, Babism, Quraniyoon (that was a new one to me), Islam (and numerous subdivisions: Ahmadiyya, Sufi, Shia, etc.), Shabakism, Meivazhi, Yazdânism (I had never heard of some of these)... The list was considerable and overwhelming. It was like a whole supermarket of religions, with shelves filled with a bewildering array of flavors and tastes. A spiritual smorgasbord! I was dizzy reading the titles of all the books on the shelves.

I finally found a good book by a popular Christian author for my wife, and as I was paying for it at the counter I shared my bewilderment over the "deli-counter" choices of spiritual books and topics with Cathy.

"Oh yes," Cathy said with pride. "We have a wide assortment of all the faiths and philosophies that are out there."

"But it all seems so confusing," I insisted. "Trying to decide and choose which spiritual direction you should take. It's almost like trying to decide which soft-drink flavor to get: cherry, grape, cola, crème vanilla, orange... It's just so much to choose from."

"Well, the world is filled with all sorts of people," she said.

I had heard this before, from Jesus himself. "Yes," I agreed. "But there should only be one Truth. How can there be so many different flavors of the truth? I mean, you can go with the 'off-the-shelf' religions such as Christianity, Islam, or Judaism—but even these come in dozens of flavors and varieties. Or you can go to the spicy section for a bit of Eastern Mysticism seasoned with some Jainism and a dollop of Taoism on the side…and who knows what you've got then!"

Cathy looked a bit puzzled at my vehemence. "Hey, whatever floats your boat!"

I knew Cathy had to deal with all sorts of patrons and customers, so of course she would have that attitude (she did own a business after all). But I was curious about her own personal feelings. "But what do you believe Cathy?" I asked.

"Oh," she said, a bit embarrassed. "I don't go in much for all that spiritual stuff. I just try to get by. You know, live and let live."

"You don't subscribe to any specific religion?"

"No, not really," she replied. "My husband was raised a Catholic, but my parents weren't very religious, so I have no real religious notions or predispositions."

"Do you read those types of books at all?" I asked.

"Sometimes," she said. "But mostly so I can keep up with what's popular. A lot of that spiritual stuff is very trendy right now. Some of my best customers come in for those types of books, so it pays to know what my customers are reading."

"And do you have any thoughts on the books you've read?"

She thought for a moment. "No, not really. I find it all very confusing most of the time. If God's that complicated, I'm not sure I even want to figure Him out."

That last statement from Cathy shocked me into silence. I paid for the book, said good-bye, wished her well and a merry (early) Christmas, and I left.

Of course the next morning I brought the subject up with Jesus.

"Good morning Jesus."

"Good mornin' Rob." Jesus said. "How are you today?"

I told Jesus about my visit to the bookstore and about my thoughts on the smorgasbord of religious and spiritual material available to the consumer today. "I couldn't get over how many different religious and spiritual books are available these days. It was like cafeteria-style religion: just take a taste of that and a dab of this..."

"Yes," Jesus said sadly. "I'm sure the supermarket of religions looks very attractive to people, especially in this culture. You folks like your choices; you're all individuals. But the danger of this post-modern approach to religion is the 'feel good' syndrome again: if it looks good, and feels good, and it seems to work for you, then it must be true. But at the end of the day, what people need to realize is: there is only one Truth."

"That's what I said to Cathy, the owner of the store: there should only be one Truth."

"Yes! And I do not want anyone becoming a Christian simply because my way _feels_ better or seems more satisfying or more fulfilling than those other philosophies. No, I want people to follow me because I have the Truth. Perhaps it would be useful if people were, in this sense, like your scientists. You don't have to stop thinking; it's not necessary to turn off your brain. My followers should be inquisitive: they should, perhaps, tryout several theories to see which one is really true before they devote themselves to me. No one devotes themselves to what they think is a lie, and I want my followers to come to me because they know in their hearts that I have the _Truth_. Not because I make them feel good or Christianity interests them where others don't. No, it's very important that people know the Truth."

Of course I agreed whole-heartedly with Jesus, but the truth can get lost in all that other stuff. "But there are so many spiritual philosophies to choose from," I lamented. "I was comparing the multitude of alternative books to the Bible section in the store, and there seemed to be more copies of those other religious books from other philosophies than there were Bibles. How can we convince people that the Bible is true? I mean, compared to all those other books on the shelves?"

"Well, we can start with the fact that the Bible is the true revelation from my Father. The Bible reveals God."

This was all well and good, but I had had this discussion with others several times, and I saw a problem. "But Jesus, we're just mortals. How can humans really expect to know God?" This was a question that was often put to me when I was trying to convince people of the truth of the Bible. And it was a valid grievance, I thought.

"That's a good question Rob," Jesus said. "You always ask the big questions! But let's not start there; let's start with something easier, like: 'What did you have for breakfast this morning?"

I didn't understand. "What do you mean?"

"I mean," Jesus said, "that I'm interested in finding out what you had for breakfast. Now, I could sit here and guess, 'Did you have cereal? Did you have eggs?' Someone might even tell me that this morning you had last night's left-over lasagna, but does that make it true?"

I still wasn't sure what Jesus was getting at. "Huh?"

"Don't you see?" he asked. "That's the same way a lot of people go about trying to know my Father. They try to guess what God is like. They'll say things like, 'Well, I like to think of God as...' and you fill in the blank."

"Okay..." I said, trying to follow his logic.

"Come on Rob!" Was it possible that Jesus was becoming just a little frustrated with me? "The only real way for me to truly find out what you had for breakfast, since I wasn't there with you, is to <u>ask you</u> to tell me. Right?"

"Right, but..."

"No 'buts'!" Jesus said. "That's the only real way. So it's dumb to sit around guessing at it. Likewise it's dumb to try to guess what God is like. It would be much better to get my Father to actually tell you what He is like. And that's what the Bible does: it tells you about my Father. God has revealed Himself to you in the Bible."

It was becoming clear, sort of, I think. We, that is Christians, believe the Bible is the revealed word of God—God's truth so to speak—because Jesus himself believed this. To Jesus, the Bible was the last word to end any argument. It was the Truth.

"I remember reading something about that in the New Testament," I said. "In the Book of Timothy, Paul said: 'All

Scripture is God-breathed and is useful for teaching, rebuking, correcting and training in righteousness (2 Tim 3:16).'"

"Yes, that's it exactly!" Jesus said. "The difference between the Bible and those other religious texts is that the Bible is 'God-breathed.' Even though it was written over many centuries and has 66 books in it, there is a unity of purpose to it because it really has only one divine Author: my Father in Heaven."

"And that's why we're not really free to just pick and choose the parts we like over the parts we don't like," I added.

"That's right," Jesus said. "Oh, I know it's tempting to pick just the bits you agree with and like. Even my disciples didn't like it when I spoke about God's judgment. They much preferred it when I spoke about God's love. But they had to take the parts they liked with the parts that were not so agreeable to them."

"Kind of like a biography that includes not only the likeable aspects of a celebrity but also the bad-but-true things that everyone has in their lives as well, warts and all," I said, attempting to paraphrase again.

"Well, sort of," Jesus said. "But of course my Father doesn't have 'warts.' It's all good, but some people might not like or agree with the reality of my Father or His designs for them. But the Bible tells you the real story of our relationship with God. It reveals God's character and it reveals His will for us."

"But to a lot of folks the Bible is a bit dry and a little wearisome to read. Sometimes it appears to be just a bunch of dogmatic propositions in a boring text book."

"Rob, are we talking about the same book?" Jesus asked.

"I think so. Why?"

"Because the book I'm talking about is full of poetry, description, letters, proverbs, stories, history, speeches and some of the finest literature ever written. It has to be that diverse because it's bringing the story of God's relationship with humanity in all its various and vibrant aspects. There's no other book like it!" he said.

"Okay, okay," I said. "Maybe not the best choice of words on my part. But what about the more difficult parts of the book, the more fantastic? That's a big sticking point with a lot of people. Some things in the Bible, like Creation for example, are just too fantastic to believe for a lot of folks."

"And those other books you mentioned, from other religions…" Jesus said. "They don't include anything, as you said, 'fantastic'?"

"Well, sure, I guess," I stammered. Although I consider myself fairly well-read, I have only explored a few of those other religions and philosophies; others I have really only perused a bit. But I was fairly sure they included some unbelievable items. "But how do I respond to people who object to all the unbelievable and fantastic things they read in the Bible?"

"Well, first I think you should use a different word. When you say 'fantastic' I think you referring to fantasy, as in made-up. That's not the Bible. The Bible is true; it just has some hard-to-believe information in it."

I wasn't sure Jesus was following me. "I was talking about the stuff we humans find so hard to believe, like the creation story, or your virgin birth, or the story of the flood, those kinds of things."

Jesus nodded. "Yes, I know you people have some trouble along those lines. But that's because you're all such intellectuals; you want everything to be logical and intuitive. But not everything is logical and intuitive. Take Creation. It's very complicated, as you can probably guess. The story is full of not-so-easy to understand truths. The best way to communicate these not-easy-to-understand truths, as some of your better writers have discovered, is through the use of metaphors."

"Metaphors?" I repeated.

"Yes, quite so," Jesus said. "Try to picture a small insect, say an ant, trying to comprehend the Empire State Building. He might say to the other ants, 'Hey, I just saw the biggest ant hill I've ever seen!' Now, technically the ant is completely wrong: the Empire State Building is nothing like an ant hill. But from the ant's point of view, the only way he has to describe it to other ants is to say it's an incredibly huge ant hill. From the ant's perspective, that's a true statement. But from ours, it's wrong."

"So we're all like ants trying to figure out the Empire State Building?" I suggested.

"Sort of. There are very complicated stories in the Bible, and they are not just trying to give you the facts of the story line so you have an interesting plot to read. No, their purpose is much deeper than that. A metaphorical story can contain many important truths, but they're hidden, or rather artistically interwoven in the other elements of the story. Do not dismiss the more implausible stories in the Bible. They sometimes have larger truths in them than the stories containing mere facts."

"So you're saying a lot more can be communicated sometimes by using a metaphor than by trying to say the same thing with just the facts?"

"Exactly," he said. "For instance, if I said that man over there was a brick wall, you might call me on it because a man is not made of bricks and mortar obviously. But you'd be missing the deeper meaning in what I was saying. The man is as immovable as a brick wall, he is stubborn to the extreme but steadfast and reliable and could be counted on and leaned on and used for support and protection and… But isn't it easier to say the man is a brick wall?"

"A lot easier I guess. But the Bible is still a difficult book to read."

"Maybe it helps to think of the Bible as me sitting here speaking to you," Jesus suggested.

"That might work for the New Testament," I said, "but what about the Old Testament? It was written long before you came on the scene."

Jesus looked hurt. "I don't know why you say that, Rob, because the whole Bible is about me."

"Oh?"

"Sure!" he continued. "If you want to know me better, just open the Bible. The Old Testament is predicting me, the Gospels are revealing me, Acts is preaching about me, the Epistles are explaining me, and Revelation is expecting me. It's all about me!"

"I never thought of the Bible like that," I confessed.

"The Bible is all about the relationship you can have with me and my Father. My Father wants you to do more than just read and believe in a book; He wants to have a relationship with you, and the Bible is the handbook for that relationship. It will bring you closer to my Father. No other religion, no other way of life offers that kind of connection with God." He paused briefly, remembering something. "I can remember telling the Pharisees once, 'You study the Scriptures diligently because you think that in them you have eternal life. These are the very Scriptures that testify about me (John 5:39).' Yet did they ever come to me? No!"

"I guess they missed that particular point."

"Boy did they!" Jesus exclaimed. "And when people read the Bible it should be much more than just an intellectual exercise for your brain. It has to involve your heart as well. What other religion does that? Reading the Bible should be like reading a love letter."

"And the Bible can help in any number of common life problems, right?"

"True!" Jesus agreed. "Whatever problems you face in life, my Father has anticipated them and the answers are in the Bible, if you just know where and how to look. My Father wants to talk to you about them; in fact, He's eager to discuss your problems with you. It's all done through the Bible, and prayer."

"I guess that's why the Bible is so uniquely precious to us."

"Number one best seller for centuries!" Jesus said. It's the closest I've ever seen him come to being prideful.

I remember looking up that particular statistic for my pastor once. There are approximately 44 million Bibles sold worldwide every year. That's some best seller! It has been translated—the whole Bible—into 371 languages, and over 2,000 countries have some parts of the Bible translated into other material. Shakespeare, by comparison, has been translated into about 60 languages, and the Islamic Koran has been translated into approximately 128 languages. So the Bible is a uniquely popular book, as well as being powerful and precious.

"So if we want to know God," I concluded, "if we want to enter into a relationship with Him, then we have to interact with the Bible. No other book, or collection of books, is quite like it in the world."

"Couldn't have said it better myself!" Jesus said.

INTERLUDE

Thanksgiving was coming, and I was sitting on the porch trying come up with my yearly "Gratitude List": the things I should be thankful for this year. I say "should" be thankful for because when you're unemployed with no prospects and things are financially grim you don't feel as if you have a whole lot to be thankful for. But I was making my best attempt at it, as tough as it was.

Jesus was quietly rocking in the chair next to me. I didn't want to mention anything about the list I was composing to him because I felt I should do it on my own. But I was having trouble.

"If you screw up your face any more you're going to get a headache," Jesus commented, interrupting my musings. I must have been concentrating too hard; it affects my facial features when I think too earnestly about something.

"I'm just trying to come up with a list of things I'm thankful for," I admitted to Jesus.

"For Thanksgiving you mean?"

"Yeah," I said. "Every year my wife and I traditionally make a gratitude list that we read out at Thanksgiving dinner to our family and friends. Only this year I'm having a little trouble coming up with things I'm thankful for, since I'm unemployed and all that. It makes the task difficult."

"I don't see why," Jesus said. "I can think of hundreds of things you should be thankful for."

"Oh, I can think of the usual things: good health, a loving wife, a roof over my head, all that regular stuff. But my wife and I usually like to throw in some other things that are more specific, or more personal. But I can't think of any of those sorts of things."

"Like what?" Jesus asked.

"Well, things like: 'I'm grateful for having a good job.' Can't say that this year. Or: 'I'm grateful we got a new car this year,' which we couldn't get, of course, because we're broke."

Jesus pondered that for a second. "Seems to me you might be feeling a little sorry for yourself, Rob."

What could I say? He found me out. "You're right! I <u>am</u> feeling a bit sorry for myself. I've had six jobs in so many years. The economy keeps tanking and I keep getting laid off when it does. If I had a steady job I'm sure I could think of all sorts of things to be thankful for." I was becoming slightly impatient with Jesus for not sympathizing with me.

Jesus just sat and smiled. After a few moments I relented. "Okay," I said. "I'm sorry for that outburst, but I really can't think of a gratitude list in the mood I'm in right now. Sorry."

Jesus put his hand on my shoulder. "You don't have to apologize to me, Rob," he said softly. "But you're thinking is all wrong. You just lack perspective."

"Perspective? Again?"

"Yes, perspective," Jesus repeated. "If you think about it, there are so many things you should be thankful for, so many blessings, I doubt you could list them all."

I was just sitting there silently, hoping Jesus would offer some good suggestions. When the silence became prolonged, Jesus finally broke it.

"Rob," he asked quickly, "do you have food in your refrigerator?"

That was a strange question. "Yes, I do," I answered.

"And do you have clothes in your closet?"

"Well, yeah."

"And you already mentioned you have a roof over your head, right?"

"Yes." This was a bit monotonous.

"Well then," Jesus said, "you are richer than 75% of the people in the world."

That had not occurred to me. "I am?"

"Yes, you are," he said. "And do you have any money at all in the bank?"

"Well, yeah, we always keep something in the bank."

"And how about in your wallet? Do you have any cash in your wallet right now?"

I took out my wallet from my back pocket and opened it. "I have seven dollars in my wallet," I told Jesus.

"And I know you and Lucy have a large dish in your bedroom where you keep spare change, right?"

"Yes, we do," I corroborated.

"Okay then," Jesus said. "You are in the <u>top eight percent</u> of the world's wealthiest people!"

"Really?" There were <u>that</u> many poor people in the world?

"You mentioned your health," he continued. "You seem to be in fairly good health. Do you know that means you're better off than the nearly one million people who will die this very week out there in the world somewhere?"

That gave me pause. "I guess I should have known that, if I thought about it."

"And you <u>should</u> think about it!" Jesus affirmed. "Another thing: if I'm correct, you've never had to go to war, have you?"

"War?" I said incredulously. "No, I was never even in the military."

"So you were never captured or imprisoned? You were never tortured? Never starved?"

"No, of course not," I said anxiously. "Nothing like that."

"Good! Then you're ahead of millions of people in the world who have to go through that all the time."

"That many?"

"There's a lot of bad stuff going on out there," Jesus said. "Oh, and your church... In this country you can attend the church of your choice without the fear of harassment, or arrest and torture, unlike the millions of people in the world who face that horror every day."

"Really?" That's <u>a lot</u> of people.

"Religious freedom is actually pretty rare in the world," he said.

I was feeling like a fool. Why hadn't I thought of these things? I was so blessed, and yet I hadn't even realized it. "Anything else?" I asked.

"Sure! Both your parents are still alive, right?"

"Yeah, they're getting up there in years, but they're still going strong."

"And they've stayed married all these years?" he asked.

"Yes, they've never been divorced."

"Well, in that case, you are a very rare individual, even in this country. Most people can't say both those statements. Do you <u>now</u> realize how blessed you are, how thankful you should be?"

I saw now that I'm extremely blessed. And yet I had to have Jesus to point that out to me. I felt embarrassed at my own self-centeredness.

"I can think of at least one more thing I'm thankful for," I told Jesus.

"Oh, and what's that?"

"I'm thankful for these little chats we have on the porch! I don't know what I'd do without them."

Jesus smiled at that.

I think I'll put that one at the top of my list.

Chapter Fifteen: The Teachers

I was sitting on the porch with Jesus one Saturday morning when I saw Scott Chapman walking down the road with his wife, Gloria. They were both teachers at the high school in town: he taught Math and she taught English. My wife and I knew them from the Town Hall meetings we attended every month. They were both very civic-minded and attended the town meetings regularly.

I had spoken a few times with Scott over the years, and he always seemed to be a bright and interesting young man. Both he and his wife were in their 30s, but I remembered him telling me he did not go to any particular church. I had extended an invitation to our church, of course, but we had never spoken of it after that. I thought I might try again now, if I could call them over to the porch.

They were walking hand-in-hand on the sidewalk that passes by the side of my house (how cute!), so when they were within shouting distance I called to them.

"Hey!" I shouted, "Scott, Gloria! Feel like coming over?"

They had been talking intently between themselves, their heads down and close to each other, when I called to them. They looked up searching for the direction of the voice that had called, and saw me waving to them from my porch. They smiled and started to come over to the railing.

"Don't you two look like the perfect couple," I said as they came over. "Just going for a walk?"

They both smiled at me. "Yup!" Scott said. "Such a beautiful morning, the wife and I decided to get a little exercise and walk into town."

"It was too nice a day to take the car," Gloria added.

"It sure is," I agreed. Then I decided to enquire further. "I was going to ask you if you would like to come to our church next Sunday." There, I popped the question.

They both blushed slightly. "Gee, thanks Rob," Scott said a bit uncomfortably. "But Gloria and I aren't what you might call 'church-going' people."

"What do you mean?" I asked.

'We're not very religious," Gloria offered.

Jesus was sitting in his chair on the porch while I was talking to Scott and Gloria. So far he hadn't said a thing. Suddenly he piped up.

"That's nice. Neither am I," he said.

This statement from Jesus surprised me so much I forgot Scott and his wife knew nothing of the chair for Jesus on my porch, so when I turned to address Jesus they must have thought I had lost my mind. "That's a strange thing for you to say," I said to Jesus.

"Why?" he asked.

"Who are you talking to?" Scott asked. I was right. Both Scott and Gloria were looking at me as if I were nuts.

So I explained about the chair for Jesus and how I spoke with him most mornings right here on my porch. I'm not sure they understood the whole thing, but they accepted it.

"And he's sitting here now?" asked Gloria.

"Yup!" I said. "He's right here in this rocking chair. He was listening, and he just said something."

"What did he say?"

"He said: 'That's nice. Neither am I' after you said you weren't very religious."

The blank look on both their faces told me what I had suspected. They thought I was in la-la land.

Scott looked puzzled. "Why would Jesus say something like that?"

"I'm not sure," I answered. I looked toward where Jesus was sitting. "Why did you say that?"

"Because Christianity is not a religion," Jesus answered.

Now, let me tell you something about Jesus. Anyone who says they know what Jesus would say in any given situation is sadly mistaken. Jesus will surprise you every time. Just ask (if you could) any Pharisee he ever spoke to. Or ask the Apostles. Jesus was always saying the unexpected, and this was a perfect example.

"You're going to have to explain that," I requested.

"Okay. The reason I say Christianity is not a religion is because it's a <u>life-style</u>, not a 'religion' as religions of the past were defined."

"How so?"

"Well, religions have always had intermediaries, priests or shamans who interceded with the god or gods on behalf of the people. They were the go-betweens; theirs was the job of taking the people's prayers, petitions and sacrifices to the god-head and making the offerings to that god-head so he wouldn't smite the people. With Christianity you don't need any intermediaries...you have me! Christianity is more of a lifestyle than a traditional religion. All the sacrifices have been made, there are none needed anymore. You can come directly to me; you don't need a priest or shaman to do it for you. Traditional religions require continuous supplication to the god-head. Christianity only requires loving God and your neighbor. Religion compels obedience and ritual; I ask my followers to serve everyone. Religions tend to exclude people and separate everyone into 'us' and 'them.' Christianity wants to include everyone, so that everyone can become 'us,' with no 'them.'"

I repeated what Jesus had said for Scott and Gloria.

"Interesting," Scott said. "I have never heard <u>that</u> description of Christianity before."

"So why not come to church and find out a bit more?" I suggested.

They were both shaking their heads negatively. "No, we're not church people," Gloria said. "We're just teachers. We belong in a school, not a church."

"Oh, that's where you're mistaken," Jesus interjected. "The church is very much a school. In the New Testament there are hundreds of references to learning, teaching, and instruction. In the Bible, when the word 'church' is used, it always means 'people.' Not a building, but the people. And what are these people? They are <u>students</u>, learning about me. Wouldn't this suggest that a church is very much like a school?"

I was echoing what Jesus said for the benefit of the Chapmans, since they couldn't hear him. "Is that so?" Scott said suspiciously. "So Christians are actually teachers?"

"Sure," Jesus said. "So much attention has been given to the learning part of being a Christian that we often forget there is also a teaching part as well. When I chose my apostles they had basically two things to do: to be with me, and to be sent out. The 'to be with me' part focuses on them being students;

the 'to be sent out' focused on them being teachers. The two go together, you know. And teaching is no less important than learning."

"I always say that," Scott said.

"No you don't," Gloria corrected him.

"Yes I do!" he affirmed.

I was getting dizzy listening to them go back and forth. Fortunately Jesus was not finished.

"What you must remember is," Jesus continued, "teaching is not just lecturing in front of a bunch of bored people in rows of desks. Teaching is an experience. Real teaching happens in many ways. And a lot of people ignore the best way: teaching by example."

"Right!" I said. "I try to do that all the time. Jesus, you taught us a way of life, and we learn it and model it for others. That's what brought the Good News down through the centuries—teaching by example, passing it down from generation to generation. You can't spread the Gospel just by talking about it and lecturing people."

"Right!" said Jesus. "I think it was Frances of Assisi who used to tell his followers: 'Everywhere you go, preach the Gospel; and when absolutely necessary…use words.'"

"I think I heard that once somewhere," Gloria said.

"But don't get the idea that we teach just as the regular schools teach," Jesus said. "No, our 'schools' are not grim places where stern teachers beat Latin verbs into little kids, or where dusty professors lecture on Plato and Aristotle. No, we do it a little differently."

"Is it a better way?" asked Scott.

"We believe it is," said Jesus. "Our teaching is not merely the intellectual transfer of knowledge under conditions of strict discipline, such as you might find at many universities. No, our way is much more like a continuous, almost unrecognized schooling that goes on in a loving family."

"In a family?" asked Gloria.

"Yes, in a family. For instance," Jesus said, "a lot of Christian learning—developing of attitudes and discussion of moral values—takes place at the <u>family meal</u>. This is why I did so much teaching at table. I told my disciples to keep meeting at the communion table, that I would be there, and the Holy

Spirit would lead them into Truth. So, around the table you share in family giving and loving, communing and singing with each other and praying for your needs and concerns. This is education at its very best."

Both the Chapmans were nodding their heads in agreement.

Jesus continued. "A child does not learn by memorizing facts. In a family children eat and drink, are loved and played with, they get kissed and cuddled, sing songs and recite jingles…long before they actually 'know' what these activities mean. In this way a child learns to copy the behavior and manners of the home—in good times and bad. The child learns to share in decision-making and moral judgments. The idea of responsibility and commitment to our family, to the Christian church and its ideals, comes later."

I could see that Jesus' words were appealing to the Chapman's attitudes about education. They seemed truly interested and maybe a bit impressed with what Jesus was saying, or rather, what I was repeating for them.

"This is very interesting," Scott said, smiling.

I just had to add my two-cents. "You know," I said to the Chapmans, "Jesus usually taught doctrines through the use of parables, and then using questions and answers."

"That's right Rob," Jesus said. "Very good!"

In years past I had been a Sunday School teacher at church; a job with many rewards. When I taught the kids, I tried to do it in a way I thought Jesus would approve. Instead of memorizing verses and creeds I try to teach the kids how to talk to God, how to tell Him their doubts and problems, how to thank Him…in short, how to have a relationship with God. I wanted to teach them how to forgive and accept forgiveness, how to love their parents, their friends, their future children…and their enemies. I tried to be practical about how each youngster could serve, how they could develop their personal gifts or talents and deal with strong emotions…all that stuff. I tied to help them find their way through the Bible for a balanced spiritual diet. Doctrine, in the sense of complex theological convictions, would come later, in a natural way. I felt that was the way Jesus would approve.

"You know," Scott said. "That's really good advice. I'd like to try it out sometime."

"Why not come to church and try it out in Sunday School?" I quickly snuck in. I was going to plug my church at every opportunity.

But Jesus wasn't done speaking. "If you think about it," he said, "my way of teaching and learning—education in a family atmosphere—is far removed from academic theology. Our schools, our church, should really have little to do with hard benches, rote learning, wearisome classes and the trauma of examinations. We just don't do it that way. They should be more like happy kindergartens."

"'Happy kindergartens,'" Gloria repeated. "I like that."

"So," I snuck in again, "how would you like to come to church next Sunday?"

"Well, maybe," Scott murmured. "But sometimes I feel like you church people think you're so much better than the rest of us. You know...the 'holy than thou' syndrome. That really turns us off."

"Oh, we're not like that at all," I reassured him.

Jesus spoke up once again. "You know," he said slowly, "too often the word 'Christian' is given quite a different meaning from what it really means. Some churches have managed to suggest that a Christian is someone who attains a certain high status, who has some special goodness, or some special mystical experiences, or has all the answers, or makes great decisions, or has a better understanding of particular doctrines... But nothing is further from the truth, really. A church is really only one thing: a group of my disciples. And my disciples are a group of <u>learners</u>. My followers, my <u>true</u> followers, are not the chosen few who have arrived, but <u>children on the path, children who are learning</u>."

I looked at the Chapmans. "So what do you say?"

"Okay Rob," Gloria said after looking to her husband. "You want us to come by on Sunday morning, or will you and Lucy pick us up?"

Chapter Sixteen: The Homeless Ones Return

It was getting closer to Thanksgiving, the weather was turning colder and the leaves were almost gone from the trees. It was a windy Saturday morning, my wife Lucy was working in the kitchen and I was out on the porch with Jesus. We weren't talking about anything in particular, just small talk, when we saw Joseph and his wife, the homeless couple, coming down the street.

I waved to Joseph and Marge and they started to come over. They seemed to be lacking the usual spring in their steps. Something must have caused their mood to darken. They came up to the porch silently. This time they didn't have their shopping cart full of paraphernalia. They seemed lost without it.

"Hey guys!" I said as they came up to the porch. "How's everything these days?"

Joseph's head was hanging low, and when he spoke it was as if he were speaking to the ground. "Had a pretty bad time of it last week," he said despondently. Marge's face never changed from her usual blank expression.

"Why?" I asked. "What happened?"

"Well," Joseph began, hesitating slightly, "I got $20 for helping this guy lay some carpeting last week, and…"

"Yes?" I inquired. He seemed reluctant to continue.

"He bought a cheap bottle of vodka and downed the whole thing in one sitting," Marge continued for him. "Had to take him to the hospital. He almost died." Marge's face was stern. Joseph was silent, his head hanging loosely from his shoulders.

"Oh no!" I cried. "Why did you do that, Joseph?"

Joseph just looked silently at me with that typical alcoholic "Why are you asking me?" expression.

"They fixed me up," he said sharply. "Only now they have me and Marge livin' in this halfway house next to the hospital, and they have me going to this out-patient group thing three times a week."

That sounded like a good thing and I told Joseph that. Marge seemed to agree, as she was nodding her head.

"Yeah, I'm off the booze for good they say," Joseph lamented. "And that guy Bob from the AA meeting they have at the Legion Hall? He came to see me when I was laid up. That was really nice of him."

"Boy I'll say!" I would have to remember to give Bob the Hat a good slap on the back for that.

"And he talked Joseph into going to the AA meetings at the Legion Hall too," Marge piped up, smiling. She may have mental health issues, but she truly wanted Joseph to get off the booze.

"That's great!" I said, and I really meant it.

"Yeah," Joseph said, "I needed to get off the stuff I guess. Not real plannin' on dyin' you know."

"And," Marge said, warming up to her speaking role, "Bob said he could probably get Joseph a job cleaning up the Legion Hall after the meetings."

"Is that right?" I asked Joseph.

"Yeah," he acknowledged. "Said he'd pay me $10 a day, and maybe later he could add some other chores to that as he came up with them."

"Well I think that's great!" I said. This is precisely what I had been hoping for Joseph and Marge. All they needed was a little help, a little hand up, which as I mentioned is much different from a "hand out."

"He might find me something to do at the hall too," Marge added.

"Better and better," I said. "Looks like this little incident of yours, Joseph, was the catalyst you needed to get you on your way."

"On my way where?" Joseph asked.

"Oh, you say that every time Joseph!" Marge scolded him. "You know what he means."

"Yeah," Joseph said unenthusiastically. "But I still don't like it."

"Well, welcome to the club of working stiffs," I said.

Joseph looked up at that. "I thought you were on unemployment?"

Ouch! Touché! "Hey, don't remind me!" Actually, even though I'm unemployed presently I still included myself in the ranks of the working stiffs.

"Well, get to it buddy!" Joseph said good-naturedly. I think he was getting a kick out of the fact that he now had a job but I didn't.

I decided to change tracks. "Hey, not to change the subject, but what are you and Marge doing for Thanksgiving Day dinner?"

"Turkey and gravy with all the trimmings down at the shelter, as always," Joseph responded. Marge nodded her head in agreement. "We do it every year."

"I heard that," came my wife's voice from the kitchen. She stepped out onto the porch and addressed Marge and Joseph. "Now I don't want to hear any of that," she said, pointing her finger at the two. "You are invited to have dinner with us on Thursday, and I don't want to hear any arguments!" When my wife used that tone of voice you did <u>not</u> want to contradict her.

Joseph looked like he had just been smacked in the face with a shovel. He had that "deer-in-headlights" look I was very familiar with, having been on the receiving end of my wife's pronouncements many times before.

Marge was smiling. "That's so nice of you," she said. "We'd be happy to come for Thanksgiving dinner with y'all." Joseph was still recovering from my wife's verbal assault.

"Good," my wife said. "Then it's settled. We'll see you both on Thursday. Why don't you come early, say sometime around one o'clock, to start on the <u>hors d'oeuvres</u>?"

"Hey, if you come earlier, at high noon, we can listen to Arlo Guthrie sing "Alice's Restaurant" together!" I suggested.

My wife just shook her head in frustration. "He does that every year. Some kind of old hippie tradition or something like that."

"Hey!" I said. "Don't knock Arlo!"

Joseph, though, was brightening up a bit. "Hey, I like Arlo Guthrie," he said. "Okay, we'll be there by noon."

"I'll have a place ready for you on the couch," I said happily. "It'll be good to have someone to watch the big game with."

"Well, why don't you invite Bob over too?" Joseph suggested. "I don't think he has any plans for Thanksgiving either."

"Hey!" I said approvingly. "Great idea!" And with that Marge and Joseph made their way back down the street to wherever they were going before they stopped by.

Jesus, who had been sitting there in his rocking chair the whole time, listening, just smiled at me. There were no words needed. Just his smile.

Chapter Seventeen: The Questioning Ones

Thanksgiving dinner went great at my house. We had Joseph and Marge, and Bob the Hat came too with his "significant other" Laura. The six of us pigged-out on turkey and all the fixin's, and it was delicious, as always. After dinner, before desert and during a break in the big game we three guys took our non-alcoholic drinks out on the porch for some air. Bob asked if Jesus would be out there on the porch as well, and I told him sure, if he liked I could ask him to sit with us a spell.

"Good!" said Bob. "I have some questions for him." This stuck me as slightly ominous. There was no telling what kinds of questions Bob would want to ask Jesus. I was a bit nervous.

When we got out to the porch and settled in our stools and chairs, Bob turned to me. "I'd like to ask Jesus some questions if it's okay?"

"Sure," I stammered nervously, "but how many questions do you have? It sounds like you have several."

"Well yeah, I do have a few." Bob gave me that look of his that could freeze ice, then he smiled. "But I can start slow, with a basic question I've been wondering about."

"Go ahead and let him ask," Jesus encouraged from his chair.

"Okay," I agreed. "Go ahead Bob, ask."

"Great!" Bob turned and looked straight at Jesus' rocking chair. "Why did you have to die back then?"

I have to admit, I was stunned by Bob's question. That question goes right to the core of our Christian belief. It was sobering to hear the question put so plainly. I looked over at Jesus to see how he reacted to Bob's question.

He seemed to be pondering the question. His eyes were closed. Then he said: "That's a really good question Bob. And to be totally honest with you, back then...I didn't know."

I was dumbfounded. "You didn't know? What do you mean you didn't know?"

When I had repeated what Jesus had answered, both Bob and Joseph looked totally confused.

"I don't mean to be a party pooper," Bob whispered, "but I was expecting a different answer."

"Yeah, so was I," echoed Joseph.

I had to admit, I too was expecting something totally different than what Jesus had answered. "Okay," I said to Jesus, "can you please explain that answer for us?"

Jesus smiled. "I was answering him as a man, not as the second person in the Holy Trinity," he explained. "And as a man, just a man, I too did not know why I had to die."

I was confused. "But that's the heart of the whole Christian message: that you had to die to save us from our sins, so we could be justified through your saving death on the cross."

"Yes," Jesus agreed, "that's right. And you know that because you have read and understood the New Testament. You've had instruction in the Christian message, going to Sunday School and all, and you've been trained to understand those lofty Christian terms like 'justification' and 'redemption' and the like. But those terms, and the understanding that goes with them, wasn't around when I went to the cross. My poor disciples had to make do with the parables and lessons I taught them, which in the large part they didn't understand. Before they had a chance to work it out, before faith and the Holy Spirit could help them, they were sorely unprepared for the theological implications of my death and resurrection. Those high-class terms I mentioned were not used back then, and the understanding of salvation through my death on the cross hadn't been worked out yet. Even I did not fully understand what was really going on."

I was finding this very hard to believe. "You mean <u>you</u> were not even sure why you had to die?"

"Yes, I was as much 'in the dark' as anyone else at the time. If you remember, when I went to the Garden of Gethsemane to pray just before they came to take me away, I prayed to my Father asking if this task might be taken away from me."

I did remember that part in the New Testament. It was in the Gospel of Luke. Jesus prayed to God that the 'cup' he had to drink from might be taken from him, meaning his death on the cross. "So you had doubts about what you were doing?"

"Not so much doubts," Jesus said, "but I was not completely sure what my Father's plan was. I was not privy to that information while I walked the earth as a man. Plus, as you can imagine, I was very frightened."

Now I know Jesus came into the world as a real human being, subject to all the weaknesses and foibles we humans are prey to, just like us. But I had not given much thought to Jesus being afraid, or unsure. "You were afraid?" I asked incredulously. "I find that hard to believe."

"Why?" Jesus asked. "I was a man, just like you, no different. I knew what I had to do, but I wished I didn't have to do it. Don't tell me you never felt like that before?"

After repeating what Jesus just said, Bob commented: "Sure, we've all felt like that, but you're Jesus, man! Jesus was brave, and he knew everything."

I thought I actually saw Jesus blush. "Well, I try to be brave, just like you and everyone else, but I was also just like you in that I was sometimes hesitant, I had misgivings, and I most certainly felt fear. And no, I didn't know everything. I gave up knowing everything when I came into the world."

That's right. In the Bible it says: "...rather, he made himself nothing by taking the very nature of a servant, being made in human likeness." (Philippians 2:7). "So you were as unaware of what was happening as everyone else back then."

"Well, not entirely unaware, as you say. But the important thing is that I didn't follow what I wanted, but what my Father wanted. 'Yet not as I will, but as You will (Luke 22:42).'"

I looked at Bob after telling him what Jesus had said. "Does that answer your question?"

"Yeah," Bob said tentatively. "I guess it does."

Joseph said: "Hey, I'd like to ask Jesus a question too."

"Okay, ask away," I said.

Joseph thought for a second and then he said: "Okay. Jesus, will there really be an end of the world? And, when will it be?"

I knew the answer to that question, and Jesus didn't disappoint me. "Ah, Joseph... The answer to the first part of your question is yes, there will be an end of days. 'But about that day or hour no one knows, not even the angels in heaven, nor the Son, but only the Father (Matt 24:36).'"

Joseph seemed puzzled over that answer, so I thought I'd clarify. "That's the same answer he gave the Apostles when they asked about the time of the Second Coming. No one knows. Only God knows."

"Oh, really," Joseph said disappointedly.

"'For you know very well that the day of the Lord will come like a thief in the night (1 Thessalonians 5:2),'" Jesus said in response to my clarification.

"Oh, okay," Joseph said. I could tell he wasn't totally satisfied with the answer. But he accepted it.

"All right," Bob interjected. "Here's another one: Are there really such things as angels?"

"Yes, there are," Jesus answered immediately.

The answer seemed to surprise Bob, but once he recovered he wanted more details. "There are? Really? What do they look like?"

"Bob," Jesus said, "they can look like anything my Father wants them to look like. But don't start imagining those silver-haired, feathery-winged creatures you see in the all that Renaissance art hanging in your museums. Those images come from the old Zoroastrian faith and other eastern cultures. What you need to understand is, every time the word 'angel' appears in the Bible it means 'messenger.'"

"Messenger?" Bob reiterated. "You mean like a currier or hotel page?"

"Yes, precisely," Jesus said. "And the main consideration they have for the way they look when they appear to humans is not to look too scary."

"Too scary?" Bob asked.

"Yes. My Father can have them appear to you anyway He wants, but mainly they try not to frighten humans too much when they do appear. That's why when they appear they usually look like ordinary men or women. And if you'll remember from the Bible, whenever they appear, the first thing they say is: 'Don't be afraid.'"

"So they try to appear as normal as possible," I interjected, trying to stay in the conversation myself and not just as an echo for what Jesus was saying.

"Yes, that's right," Jesus said. "Most times humans don't even realize they've had a visitation. But that's the way it's supposed to work. Angels are just the grunt-workers of Heaven; they do my Father's bidding. That's all."

"So what about the 'Heavenly Hosts'?" Bob asked. "Isn't there supposed to be an army of angels? Warrior angles to fight the devil's minions and all that?"

Jesus actually laughed out loud at that. "Yes, and no," he said. "I'm sure all that scary stuff in the Bible really impressed you, but as far as an 'army' is concerned…well, really! My Father can whip up a huge army anytime He wants, but it's hardly necessary. All that talk of 'Heavenly Hosts' and an 'army of angels' is just military talk to impress the natives back then."

"What do you mean?" asked Bob.

"I mean all that talk about God and His Heavenly Hosts and the rest of the military-speak in the Bible was used because that's what the people back then understood. If God wanted to impress on folks how powerful He was the most efficient way to do it was through the use of military terms and martial, soldierly words. That was the best way to impress people back in biblical times. It was almost all they understood. But of course my Father has little need for an army or host of angels. He is God after all. Nothing is beyond Him."

"So you're saying the army of angels and all that hosts of heaven stuff is just propaganda?" Bob asked.

"Well," Jesus said. "I don't think I'd call it propaganda, but essentially that's right. Call it an exaggeration if you want. But I'm sure you understand that my Father doesn't really need an army to get His way, right?"

"Oh yeah," Bob agreed quickly. "We're on the same page there."

"Good!" Jesus said.

"Why do we have to have doubts anyway?" Joseph asked. "I mean, why do some people accept all that Bible stuff and others don't? Can't God make us believe without having doubts?"

I was surprised by this question from Joseph that seemed to come from nowhere. It was more of a plea for help than a question, and it touched me to hear him blurt it out like that.

I think it touched Jesus too. He turned toward Joseph and said: "Joseph, what you fail to understand is: doubt is the handmaiden of faith. Questioning actually deepens and strengthens faith. It means you have an open mind, and are searching for the truth. If you didn't have doubts, I would think you weren't really taking these things seriously. Having doubts shows you're thinking about important stuff, and having questions shows you're intelligent and want to know the truth. There's nothing wrong with that."

"But aren't we supposed to believe certain things?" Joseph sighed. "Aren't we supposed to have certain things in our heads, and not have doubts about them?"

"Oh yes, certainly," Jesus said. "But being a follower of mine is not simply a matter of checking off boxes on a form saying you believe statement 'A' and affirmation 'B' and so forth without thinking. The kind of people I'd like to see following me are not afraid to wrestle with their doubts and uncertainties. I want people who are willing to discover my love for them on a daily basis, to fall in love with me again and again, every day. I want my followers to get up each morning and ask themselves: 'Do I really believe today?' And if they're honest and the answer is 'No'…well, that proves they're human. But if they work at it, when they can really answer 'Yes!' it's really a <u>yes</u>, and not a barely thought over agreement to religious dogma."

"So you don't just want your disciples to follow you blindly?" I clarified.

"No, not really. I'd prefer real people, with real minds that think and make decisions for themselves. My Father and I do not want automatons, so why should you act like automatons? You're real people, who think things through. For some, this is a 'no-brainer,' but for others…well, they have a hard time of it. And that's fine. The Truth is not afraid of people who think things through. They will find me eventually if they work at it."

There was an awkward lull in the conversation as I finished repeating Jesus' answer. Then Bob spoke up. "Can I sneak one last question in?" Bob asked.

"Sure," I said. "Fire away."

"Okay, here goes," Bob said as sort of a wind-up for the question. "What do you think of all those tele-evangelist and

Bible thumpers on TV and the radio, with their hi-tech megachurches and all? Do you agree with them? Do you approve of the way they're spreading your message?"

Uh oh, I thought. That was one loaded question. Even I hadn't had enough gumption to ask Jesus <u>that</u> question. I was anxious about how he would answer.

To my relief, Jesus was smiling. "Wow Bob," Jesus said. "That's one tough question. But to be honest with you, initially I really liked what those mega-evangelists were doing. I mean, back when this whole evangelical movement started—I think it started in England in the 1730s—they were doing really great things and really getting the Good News out there. But then they got too big, too successful, and things started to change."

"That's when they started using 'hard-sell' tactics, sounding more like used car salesmen than preachers, right?" I said.

"Well, more or less," Jesus said. "But as you know, power corrupts, and some of these evangelists started to get eaten up with their own importance, forgetting that it was not they who saved people's souls, but <u>my Father</u>. God simply used them to communicate with these souls. But the evangelists started to get too big for their britches, coming on too strong, and with frightening threats of Hell to scare people into believing. And as I said, I don't want my followers scared into believing."

"You want people who are seeking the truth," I concluded.

"Right! And one thing some of these mega-evangelists failed to realize was that their tactics often drove people away from me more often than bringing them <u>to</u> me. Their scare tactics tended to ostracize would-be believers, often offending many people who were simply trying to establish the truth. After several decades of that, people were starting to get the wrong impression of me and Christianity."

"I know a lot of people who criticize Christianity because they say we have an inflated opinion of ourselves," I added. "Often they say we come off as know-it-alls, acting like we have all the answers. A lot of times I hear people complain that we're argumentative, or that we believe everything comes in black and white easy answers, or that we just badger people until they agree with us."

"As usual, Rob, you've cut right to the heart of the matter," Jesus said to me, smiling. "It's the same with the hard-sell

Christians, with their TV commercial style and their 'I'm right and you're wrong' attitude. All this does is give the impression to non-believers that my followers are the wisest and most righteous people under the sun. They're not. They're just people looking for the truth. But this false impression, I'm afraid, has turned off many to Christianity."

"Why do you think they use those types of intimidating and demanding tactics?" I asked.

"The problem, I believe," Jesus said, "is that these preachers forgot that they were in the business of helping my Father save souls, not in the business of making money."

Bob grunted his agreement with that statement from Jesus.

"And they also forgot," Jesus continued, "or never learned, that 'No one can serve two masters. Either you will hate the one and love the other, or you will be devoted to the one and despise the other. You cannot serve both God and money. (Matt 6:24).'"

"That's right!" Joseph piped in. "They're all money-grubbing thieves!"

"Not all of them," I said to Joseph. "There are many honest and faithful evangelical preachers who don't use the hard-sell tactics, or they redirect their energy into revivals that generate a lot of enthusiasm for the Gospel."

"That's right," Jesus agreed. "Those loud-mouthed evangelicals are actually the minority. There are lots of good preachers, some very excellent in fact, who use kinder, gentler tactics, or as Rob said, they organize revivals, which I and the Holy Spirit love! These revivals can put the enthusiasm back into our spirituality and generate new membership for our churches, not to mention the feeling of service they instill in the congregation. We could actually use more of those types of evangelicals."

"And not the hard-sell, used car salesmen type of evangelicals, right?"

"Correct," Jesus said. "Often these mean-spirited preachers give the wrong impression of my Father. They make Him out to be a jealous, callous God who's demanding and threatens nonbelievers with hell. That's not my Father. All this does is give the wrong impression of my followers."

"And what is the right impression we should have of Christians?" Bob asked.

"I'm glad you asked that, Bob," Jesus said. "Rather than make out that we have black and white, easy answers to the big questions I would prefer they show us as explorers, questioners: asking questions and seeking out truth in all its variety."

"Okay, but sometimes those preachers make God look like a demanding, cruel parent," Bob said.

"But that's far from the truth, Bob," Jesus said. "My Father is really a sympathetic, loving parent. This image of a demanding, threatening faith is not the image I would like to see for Christianity. I would prefer showing us as self-sacrificing servers with a longing for a deep relationship with the Lord."

"That would be some difference," Bob commented. "But a lot of Christians these days say the only way you can know what God wants is to listen to them, and only them."

"But that's not correct," Jesus responded. "The way to know my Father is through the <u>Bible</u> and prayer. I want my followers to experience Him through the amazing stories that are in the Bible, through its passionate beauty, its intense poetry…"

"But they always use those 75-cent words and make it out to be so complicated," Bob bemoaned. "Sometimes they make you feel as if you're uneducated, that you don't belong."

"And it's just the opposite that I truly desire," Jesus said. "I want my followers to develop a sense of belonging to a community, with lots of different people at different levels of understanding. And you shouldn't need a formal education to be a Christian; I don't want people to think they can only know God through abstractions and complicated terms used only by theologians."

"But a lot of times these preachers seem to want absolute control over us," Bob said. "I mean, it's almost as if they want to brainwash us. And they can be pretty cold and condescending."

"But again Bob, it shouldn't be like that at all," Jesus said. "My Father is not cold, not arrogant or controlling; He's very emotional, very sensitive…actually more like an artist (just look at the landscapes!). And He's <u>passionate</u>! Especially about things like good and evil, justice and injustice."

"But what about when they say 'Believe or burn in hell!'" Joseph said. "They split everyone into 'us' and 'them' and make us people with doubts feel like outcasts. As if they don't want us."

"That's simply not true, Joseph," Jesus answered. "My Father is not biased toward anyone. As a matter of fact, my Good News is for everyone, everywhere. It does not exclude anyone, it <u>includes</u> everyone. I offer mercy and a kind of acceptance no other way of life offers today. I want 'us' to be a blessing to 'them' so we can make everybody 'us.'"

Joseph was troubled by something. "If that's the way they're supposed to act," he said, "then why don't they? Why do they always want to debate and put you in your place? Why can't they be nicer?"

"I don't know Joseph," Jesus sighed. "But what I'm suggesting is that we try to make talking about the Gospel less of a confrontation or debate, with a 'winner' and a 'loser' and an 'I'm right and you're wrong' attitude. It should be more like a harmonizing discussion, where everybody wins."

I was about to say that we had pretty much exhausted Jesus with all our questions when my wife called us in for desert. So we said good-day to Jesus, and added a happy Thanksgiving, and went into the dining room as Jesus returned to his meditation. Saved by the pumpkin pie!

INTERLUDE

After that marathon questioning session at Thanksgiving I didn't think I would have any more questions for Jesus soon, but I had thought of something I had wanted to ask but never had the chance to sneak in. So a few days after Thanksgiving I was sitting with Jesus on the porch, and I decided to ask the question I was thinking about.

"Jesus," I said as we both sat on the porch enjoying the morning, "I have another question for you."

"Another one?" he said, surprised. "You mean you have another one after all those questions on Thanksgiving? You sure do know how to wear a guy out."

"Well, this is a tough one, and I can't believe we didn't ask you the other day," I said. "It has to do with hell…"

"Oh boy," Jesus moaned. "Here it comes."

"I thought you might guess what I'm about to ask," I said. "Okay, here it goes: If God is so loving, how could He send people to hell?"

Jesus was nodding. "Yes, I've heard that question often before. First, let's clarify something. If, as you say, these people are going to hell, then they're sinners, right?"

"Yeah, as we all are, but for argument sake let's say they don't believe in you and they're sins are un-repented and unforgiven."

"Okay, so we're talking about sinners then," he reasoned. "So, are you saying it's unjust for my Father to judge sinners at all?"

"No, of course not," I answered. "It's the punishment I'm asking about. Why do people, sinners as you said, have to burn in Hell for all eternity just because they don't believe?"

"That 'burn in hell' phrase is a bit dated, don't you think?" he asked.

"What do you mean?"

"I mean, all that fire and brimstone and that suffering imagery is from another time. They used to use phrases like that to scare people into believing, and I've already told you I don't want my followers scared into believing. I used those kinds of analogies myself sometimes, as when I compared Hell with the dumping ground outside Jerusalem, called <u>Gehenna</u>. They used to throw rocks of sulfur, what was called 'brimstone' back then, into the pit to help the garbage burn. It was a horrible place, and that's why I used that imagery when I was describing hell. But it was only an analogy, one I hoped they'd understand. Today, I think it's best to picture Hell as a place where there is no presence of my Father."

I had heard this description before. I believe Jesus was saying that it was not useful anymore to think of Hell as a place of fire and torment; those images were old fashion and out-of-date as well as inaccurate. He was suggesting we simply think of Hell as a place directly opposite of Heaven, where God's presence is not manifested, even as it is in this world. To me it was hard to imagine a world where God's presence was totally unknown.

"Okay," I said. "I'm trying to imagine just such a place where God is not present, but it's very difficult."

"Just try to imagine what it would be like if you had none of the blessings you have in this world," Jesus suggested. "Only worse, because without my Father you're completely alone."

"Okay," I said. "I think I can do that. But that's exactly my point: why would God put people there after they die? It's seems unusually cruel."

"Don't tell me you're trying to judge God, Rob," Jesus warned.

"No!" I protested. "I would never do that. I'm just trying to understand why your Father would punish people so severely for just not believing in the correct things."

"You know," Jesus said, "it always surprises me how folks can talk about the 'Good News' but never expect there to be any 'bad news' as contrast. Salvation would hardly bring glory to my Father if there were nothing to be saved from, would it?"

He had a point there. If we go around talking about the Good News of Jesus Christ, there has to be bad news as well that we're trying to counter. And the bad news is: if you are not saved by God's grace through Jesus, you're going to hell. But that still bothered me.

"But who, exactly, are we talking about?" I asked. "Seems to me that most people, if they understand the alternative, would not choose to go to hell."

"I know this is hard for you to understand, Rob, but there are people who do not love my Father. In fact, there are some who actually hate God."

That <u>did</u> surprise me, but it shouldn't have. I sometimes think the world is only populated with people just like me. Nothing could be further from the truth.

"I know that what you say is probably true," I said to Jesus. "It's just hard for people like me to comprehend."

"Well, in a way, that's good. But there <u>are</u> people who sin because they want to. Sometimes they even decide to consciously hate my Father. Oh, they know of Him, but they hate Him, just like Satan. And most of the time these same people who hate my Father are the ones who complain that He's not a loving God because people like them go to Hell. But they choose Hell of their own volition."

"There are really people like that?" I asked. I just couldn't fathom it.

"Yes, there are. Oh," Jesus added, "then there are the ones a lot of folks would consider evil even in today's world: murderers, rapists...you know, criminals who never seem to get punished in this life. Most people know that it's wrong these criminals are never brought to justice, never made to account for their sins. Most good people's hearts demand justice for such evil. Hell is my Father's answer."

"But those are people who deserve Hell," I protested. "What I'm asking about are the people who aren't necessarily evil, they simply don't know about you."

"I thought I cleared that up when we talked about the Book of Revelation," Jesus said. "I think we should limit this discussion to those who are blatantly against me and my Father, and let God handle the fringe folk."

Fringe folk. I liked that. But he was right. My question about Hell is not about those who haven't heard of Jesus, or who don't believe in him for one reason or another. No, I reckon my question about Hell actually had to do with truly evil people, who consciously do wrong and go against God.

"Okay, I see what you mean," I said. "You're saying that Hell is a place without the presence of God, and that it's a place in the afterlife where truly evil sinners go because they can't go to Heaven, right?"

"Now you're starting to get it," Jesus said.

"I seem to remember you saying something about weeping and gnashing of teeth when you talked about Hell in the New Testament," I said.

"That's correct," said Jesus, reaching for the Bible I kept on the porch and opening it up to the Gospel of Matthew. "Here, in Matthew 13:42, I said: 'They will throw them into the blazing furnace, where there will be weeping and gnashing of teeth.'" He flipped to the Gospel of Luke. "I said pretty much the same thing in Luke13:28: 'There will be weeping there, and gnashing of teeth, when you see Abraham, Isaac and Jacob and all the prophets in the kingdom of God, but you yourselves thrown out.'"

"What, exactly, did you mean by 'weeping and gnashing of teeth'?"

"Well," Jesus said, "when do you usually weep and gnash your teeth?"

I had to think about that. "I don't know," I said, still thinking. "Maybe when I'm angry?"

"No, I know you, and you yell and scream and wave your arms in the air when you're angry. Not much weeping and gnashing of teeth going on when you're angry."

"Okay," I said. "How about when I'm sad?"

"You may weep a bit when you're sad," Jesus replied. "But I don't remember you gnashing your teeth."

"So?" I said, giving up. "When would you say I weep and gnash my teeth?"

"When you're frustrated, Rob."

Ah, frustration. Jesus was right about that. When folks get frustrated, they do tend to grind their jaws and gnash their teeth. It's a natural response. "So you're saying that people in Hell will be frustrated?"

"Totally frustrated," Jesus said. "They will know what they could have done to escape Hell. They will understand the love God offered to them, and how they rejected it. After they've died, when they're finally in the pit and there's nothing they can do about it anymore, they will finally comprehend that they had made the wrong choice in life, and their frustration will know no end. <u>That's</u> what Hell will be like."

"But does God really send these folks to this awful place?" I asked.

"You know," Jesus mused, "it's strange the way unbelievers will talk about how horrible it is for God to send people to hell. They make it sound as if the whole world were full of innocents (like themselves I guess they mean). But I can assure you, Rob, there will be no innocents in hell. Those who go there will be anything but innocent."

"Okay," I agreed. "But what about the lesser sinners? Those who don't believe in anything but live a moderately good life anyway. Will they also go to hell?"

"Rob," Jesus explained, "if someone robbed your home or you were the victim of some other crime against you, you'd demand justice. You'd insist the guilty person pay for what he or she did to you. Well, each time someone sins it's an affront to my Father, and justice is demanded. Believing in me is a way of atoning for your sin, through me. For folks who don't believe, well...they don't have me, do they? So they have to pay for their sins. If you've ever said, 'That person must pay for what he did!' then you're basically agreeing with my Father's concept of Hell."

"Okay, I think I'm beginning to understand," I said slowly. "But even if I agree that Hell is necessary, and provides justice for truly evil people...we're not really talking about your regular 'Joe' here, right? I mean, your average guy walking down the street isn't Hitler, or Stalin...or Jeffrey Dahmer, right? So there shouldn't really be all that many people deserving to go to hell?

Jesus looked at me; his deep brown eyes taking on a serious gleam. Again he reached for the Bible I kept on the porch. He opened it and read from the passage he was looking for: "'There is no one righteous, not even one. There is no one who understands, no one who seeks God. All have turned away, they have together become worthless; there is no one who does good, not even one.'" (Romans 3:10–12)

Yes, I knew this verse well. What Jesus was saying was: no one was really innocent. We all deserve to go to Hell. If we reject God's offer to be with Him, then something else must become of us. If someone decides in such a way, then God really has no choice. Of course we all find the thought of eternal nothingness without God to be distasteful. Who would want anyone to spend eternity trapped in such a place? But if you reject God's grace through Christ, what else is left? Because we have free will, we can choose to destroy ourselves, God will not interfere. Or we can look to Jesus for life everlasting. The choice is ours.

"Thanks for helping me with that tricky question," I said to Jesus.

"Hey," he said, patting me on the back. "That's what I'm here   for."

Chapter Eighteen: The Hopeless One

For a change—and a chance to get out of the house—I decided to go down to the local unemployment office and see if I could speak with a career counselor or someone who might help in my job search. It sometimes helps to speak with a real person and get them working on your side instead of sticking just to the internet. I drove to the state unemployment building downtown and actually found a parking spot close to the door (that probably used up all my luck for the week).

Going in through the swinging glass doors I went immediately to the "Help Desk," which exists solely to direct you to the correct line after that for what you need. Following the directions I got there I made my way to the corner offices where the career representatives were located and got on the long line leading up to the front desk. This line was merely to register on a list, a clipboard chained to the counter, so they could take you in the order you signed in. Then you sat and waited, if you could find a seat. I had a novel with me for just such a situation.

I got through the registration line faster than I had anticipated, but that probably meant I was in for a long wait before seeing a job counselor. I finally found a seat next to a scruffy guy who seemed older than me (and I usually thought I was the oldest person on the unemployment line). I sat down next to him and opened my novel to begin reading. He nodded to me in a friendly gesture, and I noticed he didn't have anything for himself to read, not even a magazine, which most people in the waiting section had in their laps. So I closed the book and turned to the gentleman, not wanting to seem as if I was ignoring him.

"Nice day today," I said, the usual small-talk.

"Yeah, guess it is," was all the gentleman said.

"Probably rain later though. It's that time of year," I continued.

"Yeah, probably," he muttered.

I wasn't sure, but it seemed he was not in the mood for conversation. So I gave up and opened my book to where I had placed the bookmarker.

"Used to work in a machine shop," he said suddenly.

I closed my book again and turned to look at the man. He was definitely older than me, and that meant he was probably retirement age. I wondered why he was down here at the unemployment office.

"You were a machinist?" I asked.

"Yeah," he answered. "Used to work in the plant downtown, until they laid me off. Tried to keep up with the changing times, but it was hard. Used to make all the fittings myself, set up the lathes to cut the material, and I also checked the parts on the machine before they went to inspection with micrometers and such. I was one of the best back then. Those were the days…"

Something about the way he spoke made me feel deeply sorry for him. "So things changed?"

"Yeah. First they went automated. Made me learn the machine language, as they called it. Just a bunch of gobbledygook as far as I could see. It was tough to learn…but I did, and they put me upstairs making the programming tapes for the NC machines. Then they came out with that 'C' language, so I had to learn that. Then they upped it to 'C Plus' and then to 'C++' and by that time I had lost count. I tried to tell them that I could pick up the new changes if they'd just give me a few weeks on the machine to learn them, but the economy tanked and they laid me off."

A sad story indeed. But that didn't explain in my mind why this old-timer was down here. Was he looking for a part-time job to augment social security? Or had I misjudged his age?

"So are you down here looking for part-time job?" I asked.

He looked up at me and frowned. "You think I'm too old to be lookin' for a real job, is that it?"

"No," I said, trying to hide my embarrassment. "I just figured you had retired and…"

"'Fraid the wife and I didn't prepare as well as we should've for retirement," he lamented.

I could sympathize. My wife and I were finding out all too well that's it's very difficult to save for retirement when you are unemployed every year or so. You have to keep hitting your savings just to pay the bills. It can be very difficult.

The man's head was hanging low, and I could barely hear what he was saying. "But there's no call for machinists like me anymore. And nobody wants to hire an old coot like me to work on these new computer controlled machines, so I have to look elsewhere for work. The wife and I can't live on what social security is sending us each month. She's already a greeter down at the mart, and I'm here lookin' for whatever I can find. But I ain't findin' nothin'!" he almost spat on the floor. "Except for sales callin' on the telephone, and I ain't gonna do that!" He slapped his knee as he shook his head briskly.

I didn't know what to say. "Sorry for your misfortune," I mumbled a bit lamely. That even sounded contrived to my ears. "But you shouldn't give up hope. Maybe something will come up that you never expected."

The man looked at me with sad eyes. "Hope," he repeated. "That's a word I haven't thought about in a long time. No, I don't believe there's any hope for folks like me these days."

I hated to hear anyone sound like that. I mean, when bad times hit, without hope…what else do you have? "Don't lose hope, sir," I tried to console. "Things will continue to change, and maybe they'll change in your favor."

"Yeah, right," he said insincerely. "But don't listen to me young man… You're the one who shouldn't give up. There's still hope for young people like you."

It had been a long time since anyone had described me as a "young person." I was overwhelmed with sympathy for the old guy. But I had no words of encouragement to tell him that would mean anything.

He feel silent, and shortly after that my name was called to talk to the counselor. But I couldn't forget my conversation with that hopeless gentleman. So naturally I told Jesus about it the next morning.

"Good morning Jesus," I said as I came out to the porch the next morning.

"Good morning Rob," he answered. "Beautiful morning, don't you think? I love these fall mornings when the trees are all in different colors and there's a brisk breeze blowing."

Actually I thought it was a bit chilly on the porch, but Jesus seemed warm enough. I had my wooly sweater on to cut the chill. So I sat down and reviewed the conversation I had with the old man down at the unemployment office with Jesus.

"That's a sad story," Jesus commented as I finished my narration.

"Yes, very sad," I agreed. "And it worries me because it's very similar to my story."

"But you'll have better luck finding a job Rob. Always keep a positive attitude, right?"

"Right!" I agreed immediately. "But that poor guy seemed so hopeless. You should've seen him: his face was lined with years of worry and stress, and he had what looked like a permanent frown. He appeared so dejected and lost."

"Yes, it's terrible when people lose hope, but apparently it happens when things keep getting worse."

"I know," I said. "I try very hard to keep the hopelessness at bay and the depression that can come with being unemployed down to a minimum. I'd like to think that I haven't lost hope yet."

"Oh, I'd say you seem hopeful enough, Rob. Looks as if you're holding the depression back fairly well."

"Yeah, I believe hope is a precious commodity to be protected and nurtured. Like my hope for eternal life with God."

"That's wonderful," Jesus said. "But of course the hope we were just talking about is not Christian hope."

"Huh? What do you mean?"

"The hope you and that man you met at the unemployment office were talking about…that's just <u>regular</u> human hope. The hope you just mentioned, the hope of eternal life with my Father…well, that's another thing altogether."

"It is?"

"Yes, it is," he said. "The hope you have in me and the saving grace of my Father is not like the hope you have for earthly things, such as hoping for a good job. You may get a good job, but then again you may not. Hoping in this case is merely wishing."

"And the hope I have for eternal life with God through your death on the cross… That's not wishing, is it?"

"Certainly not," he said adamantly. "Christian hope might share some aspects with regular human hope, but it's basically very different."

"How so?"

"Well, with human hope you might hope for good weather, but since you can't control the weather you know it might also rain. You could be wrong. Just as with finding a job. You might hope to find a good job, but you know that you may not. There's an element of the unknown associated with human hope. Christian hope is not like that. With Christian hope you really have a 'confident expectation,' a certain assurance about the things that have been promised to you, such as eternal life."

"So the hope I was talking about with that old man was not the Christian type of hope?"

"No, because when you hope in this world, you're really just imagining a positive outcome, as we discussed a few weeks ago. But that positive outcome may not happen, it may be a negative outcome that transpires, and you know this at the start with human hope. It may not work out to your advantage. In that case it's really just wishful thinking."

"But that's not the case with Christian hope?" I asked.

"Absolutely not!" Jesus said. "'There is surely a future hope for you, and your hope will not be cut off.'" (Proverbs 23:18)

I had heard our pastor talk about Christian hope, but I had never countered it against regular, human hope, and I was trying to understand what Jesus was saying. "So Christian hope is not just wishful thinking?"

"No, it is not," Jesus said categorically. "Christian hope is a direct result of your faith in me and my Father. 'But by faith we eagerly await through the Spirit the righteousness for which we hope.' (Galatians 5:5) It is a fruit of the Holy Spirit, 'Not only so, but we ourselves, who have the first fruits of the Spirit, groan inwardly as we wait eagerly for our adoption to sonship, the redemption of our bodies. For in this hope we were saved. But hope that is seen is no hope at all. Who hopes for what they already have? But if we hope for what we do not yet have, we wait for it patiently.' (Romans 8: 23-25)

"And don't forget," he continued. "Christian hope is one of the virtues of a Christian life that Paul spoke about, right there with faith and love: 'And now these three remain: faith, hope and love.' (I Cor 13:13a) Our hope is not the hope you talk about here on earth. It's a happy expectation of something that is certain. There is no doubt about it. When you hope as a Christian, you're actually looking forward to something that is absolutely true."

"I have to admit, that is much different from the hope we humans use. But the hope that the old man lost is human hope, and there's not a whole lot I can do to help him regain that hope if it's gone from him. I mean, if it's gone, it's gone."

"Well," Jesus said slowly, "when I pointed out the difference between Christian hope and regular hope I didn't mean to suggest that folks in the Bible didn't lose their earthly hope too, just as you do today; they faced failure too. And failure is what usually causes people to lose hope. As a matter of fact the Bible is full of people who failed miserably, in their own eyes. They may have thought that things appeared hopeless, but they never lost faith. And because of their faith my Father turned their failures into successes. Turns out He often uses what we consider our weaknesses and twists them into something wonderful. Consider Abraham. He was told he would be the father of a great nation, but when we're introduced to him in Genesis he's an old man with no children. As far as he was concerned life was almost over and he had no natural children. He considered himself basically a failure, and that would have been true in his culture back then, but God assured him he would father a great nation. And my Father always makes good on His promises. But at first Abraham considers himself a miserable failure. And look at Jacob, Abraham's grandson. His name means 'deceiver' you know, and that's exactly what he was: a liar and a deceiver. First he tricks his brother into selling his birthright for a bowl of soup, and then he fools his own father into bestowing his blessing—a blessing that should have gone to his older brother Esau—on him. This got his older brother so angry Jacob had to escape across the Jordan River, and when he returned he very rightly expected his older brother to kill him. But God took this trickster, this failed son and brother and made him into something great, and even gave him a new name: Israel, which his family would then use as the name of their tribe from that point on. But notice, throughout the Bible, whenever my Father wants to identify Himself to the children of Israel He always states that He is the 'God of Abraham, Isaac and Jacob'; He doesn't use Jacob's new name: Israel. He uses his old name, the name of the <u>failure</u>: Jacob. My Father wants His chosen people to know they are still His children even though they are descended from what amounted to a failure. A failure God turned into a gigantic success. So even though some may think themselves failures in this world, my Father can turn their failures into their biggest successes if they will believe and have faith in my Father's plan."

"So even our earthly failures, what we consider to be failures at least, can be made into something great by God if we only let Him work in us?"

"Yes, that's it exactly!" Jesus said. "Depression and loss of hope are endemic in today's society, and I wish those suffering people would remember that my Father is in control, and there is no failure that He cannot turn around and make right—make better even—if only they'd believe in Him and His saving grace through my death on the cross. So you see, even with regular, earthly hope, faith in me and my Father can help, if only folks would remember to look up… '"For I know the plans I have for you,'" declares the Lord, "plans to prosper you and not to harm you, plans to give you hope and a future."' (Jeremiah 29:11)

That gave me a lot to think about. "If I meet that man down at the unemployment office again Jesus," I said, "I will certainly try to tell him about all this. Perhaps he'll take heart from the Good News."

"Good! But always remember…hope is good… "But the greatest of these is love." (I Cor 13:13b)

Chapter Nineteen: The <u>Employed</u> Guy

This morning I had something really special to say to Jesus. I walked out onto the porch with my cup of coffee and cheerily greeted my Savior.

"Good morning Jesus," I said, smiling broadly.

"Good mornin' Rob." Jesus answered, smiling back at me. "You seem to be in a great mood this morning."

"That I am Jesus," I said. "I have some wonderful news!"

"Let me guess: you found a job."

"Right!" Okay, so I was a little disappointed that he guessed my news. "Found a great job with a good salary doing what I'm good at."

"But there's a catch?" Jesus asked.

"Yeah," I agreed. "One difficulty: the job is in Pennsylvania."

"And that's a problem?"

"Well, yeah, since I live in Connecticut," I said.

"Couldn't you just move there?"

"It's not as simple as that," I explained. "They want me to start next week, so I'll have to go there, get a hotel room, and come back on weekends while Lucy packs up our stuff and gets us ready to move."

"And that's a problem?" he asked a second time.

"Well, it's a major inconvenience," I amended. "Not to mention the expense of moving and all that. But we'll do it; I've already talked it over with Lucy and she agrees with what we have to do."

"Didn't you always say that you wanted to retire in Pennsylvania?" Jesus asked.

"Yes, that's why I decided to take this job and go through the whole rigmarole of moving."

"I'm sure it will all work out fine," Jesus said.

"I sure hope so," I said. "But you know what the hardest part of this move is going to be? Leaving our church family. It's going to be harder to leave all those people we've come to know and love at the church than it is to leave our real family and neighbors."

"And that's a good thing, Rob," Jesus said. "You've become so involved with your church that you're attached to all those loving people. I'm sure you'll find a good church home in your new location."

"I hope so," I agreed. "In any case, that will be our first order of business: finding a good church. We don't want it to be too big, or then they may not need us, or too small, either. But we'll find a church I'm sure."

"Well, even if it's a big church Rob, I can't see them not needing you and Lucy. You both have a lot to offer. But good luck with all of it," Jesus said.

"I was kinda hoping for your blessing," I said sheepishly.

"Okay," he said. "You want a specific blessing, or would you like the general blessing?"

"I guess the general one would be okay."

"Right!" he said. Then he placed his hand on my head as I sat in my chair, and said: "'May the Lord bless you and keep you. May the Lord make His face to shine on you, and be gracious to you. May the Lord lift up his countenance upon you, and give you peace (Numbers 6:24-26 - New American Standard Bible).'"

"Thanks Jesus," I said sincerely.

"Anytime," he answered.

Chapter Twenty: Merry Christmas!

My wife and I decided to throw a big Christmas party at our home this year, since this will be the last Christmas in our old place. We invited our friends, family and everyone we knew from church, as well as several acquaintances from town. There were more people there than I had expected. Some people we didn't even know showed up, friends of friends, etc. All in all there were a lot of people congregating in our living room and spilling out onto the porch in the moderate December air.

Bob the Hat was there, of course, with Laura his common-law wife. Mrs. Hummel came too, with a friend, a gentleman who looked to be in his sixties; seemed like a nice man. I decided to walk over to where she and her friend were standing by the bowl of punch my wife had made for the party, just to say hello.

"Well hello there Mrs. Hummel," I said as I walked up. "Who's your friend?" I was anything but shy at parties.

"Hi Rob," Mrs. Hummel said as she looked up from her cup of punch. "Such a nice house you have here. It's a shame you're leaving it." Then she must have realized she hadn't answered my question. "But where are my manners! This is my friend Paul," she gestured to her friend standing next to her. "He's with the school district. We met at the town council meeting."

"Hi Paul," I said, taking the man's hand. He appeared to be in his 60s, well-dressed and distinguished looking. "Welcome to our party."

"Glad to be here," Paul said. "Mary's right, this is a great house. I love the porch."

"Yeah, I've gotten a lot of use out of that porch in the time we've been here," (I had forgotten that Mrs. Hummel's first name was Mary.)

"Paul's a widower, and he lost his son last year," Mrs. Hummel said. "He's helping me adjust to the loss of my daughter."

"That's really great Mrs. Hummel." I was happy she had found someone who could relate to her loss and help her cope.

We all need a "help-mate" to get us through the hardest times of our lives, and I was certainly pleased that Mrs. Hummel had found someone she could talk to and share in her grief.

"Losing a child is probably the worst thing anyone can go through," Paul said. "I had a terrible time adjusting to my son's death. But with the help of God and some good friends and family to talk to, I made it through. Now all I want to do is help others to cope with losses and terrible tragedies."

"Paul hosts a counseling session at the Rec," Mrs. Hummel boasted. "It's kind of a group thing, but it sure helps to share your feelings with others who know what you're going through."

"I'm sure that's certainly true," I said. Then I saw my mother and father coming in the front door. I excused myself to greet my parents.

"Hey guys!" I called as I stepped up to take my Mom's coat and gloves. "Merry Christmas! Thanks for coming." I gave my mother a big Christmas kiss. Dad got the usual handshake.

"It's a good thing you started this soirée before it got dark," my father said. "You know I hate driving at night."

"Oh Bob," my mother scolded. "Can't you even wish your son a merry Christmas?"

"Oh yeah," my father grumbled as he took off his coat. "Merry Christmas. Here," he handed me his coat. "Go hang this up somewhere."

Good ol' Dad…grumpy as usual, I thought.

My mother, who could always tell what I was thinking, looked at me to explain. "Oh, don't think badly of your father Rob," she said. "He just sold most of his stocks online and now he has nothing to complain about."

"Wow! Is that true Dad?"

My father nodded reluctantly. "Yeah, sold 'em all. Had to. Your Mom kept saying they were giving me ulcers."

"Well they were!" my Mom said. "Those stupid stocks and all that financial mumbo-jumbo online, you were becoming a real ogre. Every day it was something else. If you hadn't stopped I would have left you!"

"Now she tells me," my father quipped. To which my mother reacted by thumping him good on his shoulder, eliciting a muffled "Ouch."

"Well, you can get your drinks over there in the kitchen," I said with a laugh, "and the food is coming any minute, so make yourselves at home…and mingle."

"Thanks dearie," my mother said, and led my father over to the punchbowl.

I saw Matt, my professor friend, talking to Joseph and Marge out on the porch. Luckily the air was relatively warm in the late afternoon, and there were a lot of folks out on the porch. I walked over to see how they were getting along.

"Yo Matt!" I said as I walked up to the trio. "So glad you could come." Matt and his wife had driven over thirty miles to be here. He was a good friend.

"Hey Rob," Matt said. "Merry Christmas!" He took my hand and gave it a good shake.

"Merry Christmas to you too," I said. Then I patted Joseph on the shoulder. "So what have you three been talking about?"

"Joseph here has been enlightening me on the Roman Empire," Matt said, barely able to hide his amusement. I was interested in how a homeless man could "enlighten" a history professor on the Roman Empire.

"Really?" I said, dubiously. "And on what particular aspect of the Roman Empire?"

"Their cuisine!" Joseph said enthusiastically. "I was just telling Matt here about the fish sauce they used to flavor almost everything they ate back then."

"Fish sauce?" I asked, puzzled.

"I believe it was called 'garum,'" Matt offered. "Joseph was telling me how they made it."

"Oh?"

"Yeah," Joseph said. "They would gut these little fish, I think they were like smelts, and put the innards in vats to ferment for weeks in the sun, until the sauce was really ripe."

"Sounds disgusting!"

"Maybe to you," Matt said. "But according to Joseph, the old Romans went crazy for it."

"Yeah," Joseph said, "it was like their ketchup. They put it on everything."

"I'll stick to ketchup," I said.

"I don't like ketchup," Marge said softly. She was certainly becoming more talkative.

"So how's the job at the Legion Hall coming?" I asked Joseph.

"Pretty good," Joseph answered. "They have me cleaning up after meetings, and now Marge is helping out in their Thrift Shop too."

"Is that right Marge?" I asked. "How's that working out?"

"Fine," she said in a soft voice.

"She really likes the ladies she's working with," Joseph offered. "And they said if I could get a driver's license they'd get me a job driving the truck too."

"That's great Joseph!" I said. Just then I saw Bob the Hat heading in our direction. He came out to the porch and smacked me on the back with a tremendous whack.

"Merry stinkin' Christmas Rob!" Bob said to me, and then turned to Joseph. "So, have you shown him your coin?"

"What coin?" I asked.

"Joe's one month sobriety coin," Bob said, looking over at Joseph and urging him to show the aforementioned coin.

Joseph self-consciously reached into his pocket and pulled out a coppery medallion about the size of a silver dollar. It had "One Month" stamped on it and had the AA triangle logo on it as well.

"Well congratulations Joseph!" I said slapping him on the back just as Bob had whacked me. "That's a real milestone. I'm proud of you!"

"So am I," Marge piped in sheepishly. She had a big smile on her face for her man.

Joseph seemed embarrassed by the attention. "Thanks," he mumbled. "But might as well congratulate me for not robbing a bank in a month too."

"What do you mean?"

"I dunno," he said guiltily. "Just seems strange them congratulating me on doing something every normal guy does all the time…or doesn't do."

"But staying away from the bottle is a real achievement for you Joseph," I corrected him. "Don't belittle your accomplishment. You've probably saved your own life doing this."

"That's what I've been trying to tell him," Bob said.

"Well thanks," Joseph timidly said. "I just wish I had started this sooner."

"Better late than never," I countered.

"Oh, by the way," Matt said to me. "I've been meaning to call you. I checked into that stuff you told me about the old myths of Horus and Osiris and all those, and it turns out…you're right!"

"I was?" I asked. "About what?"

"About the resurrection parts of those old myths," he said. "Turns out most of them had those 'coming back from the dead' parts added hundreds, if not thousands of years after the original myths were first recorded. It's very probable those resurrection endings were added _after_ the Jesus story."

I noticed he still called it the "Jesus story," but I didn't press the point. "That's what I was trying to tell you," I said. "So the gospel writers didn't necessarily copy the old stories. In many ways it was probably the other way around."

"Yeah," Matt agreed. "Makes you think, doesn't it?"

"Think what?"

Matt gave me a stern look. "Well," he said, "it makes _me_ think I may have to revisit my religious roots."

"You mean that 'old time religion' may have a few things right after all, huh?"

"Maybe…" he said, trailing off. Then he must have seen someone he wanted to talk to. "Please excuse me for a minute, will you?" he said, and was off to the living room.

Bob came over when Matt wandered off, tugging Laura behind him. He leaned in to me conspiratorially. "Hey," he said in a whisper. "I have a little news of my own."

"Oh yeah?" My curiosity was piqued. "What's that?"

"The old lady and I are tying the knot," he whispered to me. Laura, who heard Bob's failed stage-whisper, gave him a shove that nearly knocked him off his feet. She didn't like being called his "old lady."

"Say what!" I bellowed, perhaps a bit too loudly, for several people standing near us turned in our direction.

Bob smiled nefariously. "Yup! Went and got the license yesterday. Gonna make an honest woman out of her." He ducked a playful swing from Laura.

"We're gonna be married on Christmas Day," Laura added. "Can you and Lucy come?"

"We wouldn't miss it for the world," I said. "But I hope it's in the morning. We're having dinner with my folks that evening."

"Eleven o'clock in the mornin'," Bob said, "and we're being married by the pastor of <u>your</u> church, <u>at your church</u>, so you have no excuses."

"That's great Bob! I'm really happy for both of you." I was wondering why my pastor hadn't mentioned this to me. Then I realized Bob and Laura had probably wanted to keep it a secret so he could tell me himself. "Wait 'till I tell Lucy!"

"'Fraid I already popped that bubble," Laura said contritely. "I was just talking to Lucy in the kitchen, and..."

"And you already told her," I concluded for her.

"Yeah. Sorry."

"Oh, it doesn't matter," I said. "Probably better that way. She loves making a fuss over people getting married."

"Gotta run I'm afraid," Bob said. "We have to go visit Laura's father in New Rochelle. Not lookin' forward to that visit." This time the not-so-playful punch landed square in the center of Bob's chest. "Omph!" he gushed, still smiling.

"Well, God bless you both," I said to them as they were leaving. "And merry Christmas!"

Before I left the porch I saw our pastor and his wife pull up in their Honda Accord (note: not in an old beat-up jalopy like he was driving the other day). I walked around the side of the house to greet them as they exited the car.

"Merry Christmas Pastor," I said as I walked up, taking his hand in a firm handshake. "And merry Christmas to you too Melany."

"Merry Christmas Rob," Pastor's wife said. "So sad that this will be your last Christmas with us."

"Yeah," I agreed, "it's turning out to be harder to leave the people at church than we expected. But I have to go where the work is, as you know."

"Just couldn't find any work around here, could you," Pastor said lugubriously. I don't think he will <u>ever</u> forgive me for running off to Pennsylvania.

I shrugged, as we had had this conversation before. He knew very well that I had to leave Connecticut to keep working in my field.   It was just a fact of life; one he didn't like apparently.   Too many church members moving to other places.   Seems the instability was disconcerting to him.   But change is inevitable…except from vending machines!

"Is Lucy in the kitchen?" Melany asked as we three walked in the house.

"You guessed it," I said. "Where else would she be?"

As Melany ran off to talk to my wife I was left alone with Pastor in the front foyer. "I'm really glad you and Melany could come by. I didn't want to leave our conversation from the other day hanging in the air like that."

"Well Rob," Pastor said, "I've been thinking about that, and maybe I was a bit too hard on you when I criticized your talking to Jesus as a buddy."

"I know Pastor," I said. "I talked it over with Jesus (I saw him visibly cringe) and he said that as long as I keep in mind Who I am talking to, it should be okay."

The pastor smiled…a bit. "I was talking to Melany about it the other night and she scolded me for being so hard on you." I could always count on Pastor's wife to take my side in these types of conflicts. She was such a kind soul. Plus, she loved going contrary to her husband.

"So you don't think I'm committing heresy?"

He cringed again. "Not if you don't take it too far," he said.

"Thanks Pastor," I said.   I was happy he agreed with me…at least a little. I made a sincere promise to myself to make sure I didn't slack off in my awe and admiration of Jesus and his Father, God Almighty. As Jesus would say, I's all perspective…and remembering my proper place.

"Is that Dan and John from the council?" Pastor said, scanning the crowd as he hung up his coat in the hall closet.

"Yeah, they're here, and so are Tommy and Rose."

"I need to talk to Dan for a minute," he said, excusing himself.

"Just don't forget to say hello to Lucy before you and Melany leave," I requested. "I know how you two don't like to hang around at these parties too long."

"What?" he asked, chagrined. "You think this is the only Christmas party I have to attend tonight? I _am_ the Pastor of the church you know."

"Oh, I know how busy you can be," I teased him. "Places to go…people to see. So very important!"

"Your sarcasm is lost on me," he said smiling, and moved off into the crowd.

Returning to the living room I spied my cousin Johnny sitting on the sofa with his wife Irene.

"Hey Johnny!" I said, squeezing myself between him and his wife on the sofa. I turned my head toward Irene's. "Irene. Merry Christmas!"

"Merry Christmas!" they echoed in unison.

"So what are you folks up to these days?" I asked.

"Well, I've been thinking a lot about our conversation from last time," he said.

"Oh?" I replied. "And what were your thoughts?"

"After we talked the last time," he said, "I started thinking…maybe Irene and I should think about joining a church again."

"So it was you who put that thought into his head," said Irene accusingly. "All of a sudden he starts talking about looking for a church again. I told him I didn't think we were in the market after the last time. Did he tell you about that?"

"Yes," I said, "he mentioned that. But honestly, you shouldn't let one bad experience keep you from going to church. There are a lot of good churches in your area I'm sure."

"That's what Johnny was saying. But I wasn't so sure. Last Sunday we went to the Unitarian Church down the road from us, and it wasn't a bad experience for a change."

"Yeah," Johnny said. "We sat and listened to some Native American music, and they talked about love and peace and stuff like that. Wasn't bad, but it didn't seem like church, at least not as I remembered from when I was a kid."

I was glad Johnny had gotten over his aversion to organized religion, even if he hadn't chosen my church to visit at first. "So, since you've gotten one church visit under your belt, why not come to church with me and Lucy one Sunday and see what _our_ church is like?" I suggested.

Johnny paused in thought for a moment. "Hmm. Well, we'll see," is all he committed to.

"Oh John!" Irene said. "Don't put him off like that." Then she looked at me. "We'd love to come to church with you and Lucy. Just let us know which Sunday, and we'll be there." She gave Johnny a look that said: And that's the final word!

"Great!" I said. "I'll let you know." Then I tried to extricate myself from between them on the sofa, which was not as easy as I had thought.

My father was walking by and saw my plight. "Here," he said, yanking me up from the sofa with his free arm. "Let me give you a hand old man!"

"Gee, thanks Dad," I said. Old man indeed! Then I saw Nancy, the budding Buddhist, standing with my wife in the kitchen. There was another guy standing behind her who I didn't recognize, so I decided to go in and find out who he was.

"Hi there everyone," I announced as I walked into the kitchen. "Merry Christmas!"

"Merry Christmas Rob," Nancy said to me, smiling. Then she turned to the man standing behind her. "This is Ted. We meet online." I was always amazed at how many people were meeting online these days. It's not like the old days anymore, that's for sure.

"Hi Ted," I said, taking his hand and shaking it in greeting. "I'm Rob, and this is my wife Lucy," I said, gesturing to my beautiful wife standing next to Nancy. "Thanks for coming."

"My pleasure Rob," Ted said pleasantly. "Nice place you have here. But I understand you're moving to Pennsylvania?"

"Yeah, found a job in PA, so we have to go where the work is, just like my ancestors."

"I hear that," Ted agreed.

"Ted's a Baptist," Nancy said mischievously; then she added softly: "He's helping me get reacquainted with Christianity."

"A Baptist, huh?" I said, smiling and not keeping my voice down, despite Nancy's undertone. Of all the people who were here at the party, I think I was most happy to find that Nancy had found a Christian man who might help her come back to Jesus.

"Yeah, but don't hold it against me," Ted said with a grin.

I laughed at that. "I would never do that, Ted! I love Baptists. Besides, '…we preach Christ crucified…' (1 Cor 1:2a), right?"

"Right!" he acknowledged. "'…a stumbling block to Jews and foolishness to Gentiles (1 Cor 1:2b)," he added.

"So we're on the same page," I said.

"Amen!" Ted said in brotherly Christian fashion. It was as if we were having a secret conversation, one that established us both as disciples of Jesus.

"So you're not a Buddhist anymore?" I asked Nancy.

She shook her head. "Nah, I've gotten over that. It was just a fad I guess. I never really got into it very deeply. And a lot of it I just couldn't get to work for me. But Ted is helping me to understand Jesus and the Gospel message, and he makes it sound so wonderful and reasonable. He's very good at explaining things."

I was a little dejected that my explanations to Nancy were not good enough to change her path from Buddhism, but I was grateful she had found someone who could tell her the truth about Christianity, even if it wasn't me.

"I am very happy for you Nancy," I said to her. "Welcome back to the fold."

"Thanks," she said.

It was then that I saw my old friend Mike come walking in, late to the party as usual. He was bundled up for the cold, although it wasn't all that cold outside. He wore a huge, heavy parka, mittens and a scarf, which he disrobed and piled on a chair next to the door.

"Would you excuse me for a minute," I said. Then I turned to my wife. "Mike just walked in the door. I really didn't think he'd come."

"Well, you'd better go over and say hello to him," my wife said.

I walked over to where Mike was standing next to the door, still piling his vestments on the chair. "Hi Mike!" I said to him as I walked up. "It's great you could come! I really didn't think you'd make it."

"Oh, I wouldn't miss this party for the world," he said. "Didn't you say you were moving out of state next month?"

"Yup," I said. "Found a good job in Pennsylvania. I'll get a hotel room there while I'm on the job at first, and Lucy will pack up and join me in a few months. At least, that's the plan."

"I'll miss your calls and visits," he said. This touched me in ways I can't really describe.

"That's really nice of you to say," I told him. "But we won't be dropping off the face of the earth you know. I can still call you anytime, and we'll be coming back for visits from time to time, so this isn't good-bye, not really. Just 'see ya later.'"

Mike just nodded noncommittally. "I've been thinking about what you said that last time you came to see me."

He looked so despondent I was afraid I had said something that really bothered him the last time I was at his house. "Hey man, about that... I didn't mean to make you feel bad or anything. Sometimes I say stupid things."

"No," he quickly said, "you said a lot of things that were right. I do need a better job, and I do need to get myself out of this funk I gotten myself into. I just can't seem to get enthused enough to make a difference."

I felt bad for Mike. He seemed sincere. Then I saw Dorothy walking toward us. When I posted the invitation to the party on the church bulletin board, I really hadn't thought about Dorothy coming. But she came, and she was walking toward me and Mike right now. I began to sweat. But she didn't seem angry or anything, so maybe she was just coming over to say merry Christmas.

"Merry Christmas Rob," she said to me as she walked up. I was very relieved.

"Merry Christmas Dorothy," I said back to her, my fear allayed. She bent in to me and I gave her a little peck on the cheek. We do that kind of thing at our church. But she was not smiling. Not a good sign.

"I wanted to let you know that I finally got enough signatures for that petition, no thanks to you," she said off-handedly.

"I'm sorry Dorothy," I apologized. "I was really uncomfortable signing that petition."

"Yeah, I figured that's what it was," she said curtly. "But no matter. We got it done without you."

"Sorry," I repeated.

As she was walking away she stopped in mid-step, turned to me and said: "Listen, I'm organizing a group to support Senator Sommers in the next election; you know, the usual campaign work, making phone calls, shuffling paper, computer geek stuff, buttons, brochures…the whole nine-yards. You wouldn't happen to know anyone who could work until next November on the Senator's campaign, would you?"

There was a pregnant pause as I looked at Mike. Mike looked at me. Wow, talk about coincidence!

"I'm free until November," Mike murmured awkwardly.

"And who would you be?" Dorothy barked. She was usually abrupt when she spoke; a nice lady, really, but brusque.

"This is my old friend Mike," I answered for him. "We met in college way back when."

"You live around here Mike?" Dorothy asked.

"I live in Meriden."

"Close enough," Dorothy said, and took out a card from her purse. "Here," she handed Mike the card. "Give me a call tomorrow and we'll get an application over to you."

Mike took the card, looked at it quickly, then pulled out his wallet and stowed the card away. "Okay," he said as he replaced his wallet.

As Dorothy walked away I look at Mike, smiling. "Well now," I said. "Looks like you're off to the races!"

"That was kinda weird, wasn't it?" Mike said, a slight smile appearing on his lips.

"A little weird, yeah. But boy, you were just mentioning that you needed a better job, and up walks Dorothy. How about that?"

"I guess I should be careful what I wish for," he said.

"Yeah, you should," I agreed. "But remember: coincidence is merely God acting anonymously."

"I'll try to remember that," Mike said. "Where's the food?"

"Food's coming soon, but you can get a cupful of my wife's great punch in the kitchen."

As Mike headed for the kitchen, Gloria Chapman came up behind me and wrapped her hands around my eyes. "Guess who?" she asked.

I thought I'd play along. "Ah, Gloria Steinem?"

"Close," Mrs. Chapman said. "At least you got the Gloria right!"

I turned around and greeted Gloria as her husband Scott came up to us from the living room.

"Merry Christmas!" he said as he walked up and put his arm around his wife.

"Merry Christmas Chapmans!" I said to them both, giving them a double hug by trying to wrap my arms around both of them.

"Heard you're moving to Pennsylvania," said Scott.

"Yeah," I admitted. "Found a good job there. My wife and I have always wanted to live there though, so it's a good move for us."

"We'll miss you both," Gloria said. "And we have to thank you for introducing us to Mrs. Swanson at your church. We've enrolled to be Sunday School teachers there next semester. Jim's going to teach the high schoolers, and I'm taking the little ones in Kindergarten."

"That's great!" I said enthusiastically. "Mrs. Swanson never said a word to me about it."

"We didn't want to make a fuss or anything, and we wanted to let you know ourselves, so we told her to keep it on the hush-hush for now. You know, don't let your left hand know what you're right hand is doing…"

"Hey," I said. "That's from the Bible: 'But when you give to the needy, do not let your left hand know what your right hand is doing (Matt 6:3).'"

"Very good Rob," Gloria said. I turned a bright shade of red.

"Anyone need some air?" I asked the Chapmans. I was getting warm, and the Christmas sweater I was wearing wasn't helping matters. When neither of the Chapmans indicated they needed air, I excused myself to go out to the porch. As I said, the weather wasn't very cold yet for mid-December, so it was very pleasant on the porch that evening.

There were a few guests on the porch, and I greeted them politely as I stepped out from the living room. I looked over at the special rocking chair. There in the chair, smiling, sat Jesus. What a comforting sight.

"Hey everybody!" I heard my wife call from the living room. "How about we all sing 'Silent Night' together?"

People started piling into the living room from the porch, until I was left alone standing by Jesus, who was rocking gently in his chair.

"Nice party," he said to me.

"Happy birthday," I responded back.

"Thank you," he said.

I sat down in the chair next to him, and we just sat in silence for a while. Through the months we've come to an understanding, Jesus and I; we don't need to talk out loud much anymore. He knows what I'm thinking, and I know what he wants to say to me. We're comfortable in our developing relationship. I was at peace.

"Rob, you coming?" my wife called out to the porch.

"Be there in a minute," I called back.

"You'd better get in there," Jesus said. "They're going to sing 'Silent Night.'"

"It's all for <u>you</u>, you know."

"I know."

So I got up and left Jesus sitting in his chair on the porch, and went inside to sing "Silent Night."

When I got in the living room my wife—standing on her tiptoes to see me over the crowd of people waiting to sing, for she was vertically challenged—said: "It's about time you came in! You have the loudest voice you know."

"Yeah, I know," I acknowledged. I looked around at all my friends and family. How blessed I was, I thought. How wonderful it was to be alive. "So come on everybody!" I shouted. "You know the words. At least for the first verse:"

> Silent night, holy night
> All is calm, all is bright
> Round yon Virgin Mother and
> Child
> Holy Infant so tender and mild
> Sleep in heavenly peace
> Sleep in heavenly peace

"Merry Christmas everybody!" I yelled. "And happy birthday Jesus!"
"Happy birthday Jesus!" they all roared in unison.
I could see Jesus smiling and waving from the porch.

Epilogue: So Who Am I This Time Lord?

Okay…so, if you've come this far you may have guessed my secret: I have been ALL of the personalities that appear in this little book at one time or another in my life. This is actually an outline of my own spiritual journey: the peaks and valleys, the small triumphs and the big failures, the questions I've asked myself…and—I hope—some answers as well.

This entire story takes place in my mind. Understandably the words coming from Jesus are my own. That's why he speaks in colloquial English, using American jargon. In this little book Jesus talks like me. In some ways he is me, or rather my interpretation of him in my own mind. Through the years I've asked myself the very same questions you find in these pages. And I've imagined Jesus providing me with answers, or, lacking clear-cut answers, meaningful responses. I think every Christian should have this kind of relationship with their savior.

That's not to say the events and individuals displayed in this story are not real; many of the events, such as becoming unemployed, did occur. Some several times. And the people who come around to my porch do exist: there are thousands of these persons out there in the world, just as I described. Perhaps you know of one or two? Perhaps you're like someone in this little book? If so, I hope this has helped in some way.

I started this story when I was laid off my last job in Connecticut. That's all true. I was scared, and so was my wife. I did a lot of praying. And my difficulty with prayer was a real factor in the way I approached my Savior in this story. I have always spoken to Jesus as I would a friend. I have always imagined him speaking back to me as a friend, just the way he does in this little book. I wanted to put down in writing some of the lessons I had taught myself and learned, and also point out some of the pitfalls that plaque many believers all the time. I wanted to summarize some of the understanding I had acquired, and perhaps pass on a few helpful insights in the process. But make no mistake: this is <u>my</u> take on Christianity and what it means to be a disciple of Christ. I do not claim to speak for any Christian denomination or group. I merely speak as a Christian seeking Truth (with a capital "T"). This may not harmonize with your personal assessment of the Christian religion, but it's <u>my</u> understanding and I'm comfortable with it, and I believe others may find it comforting as well.

That being said, I should point out that the philosophical and religious viewpoints offered here are the result of a lifetime of research, reading and perusing untold volumes both popular and obscure, attending lectures, college courses...and talking to numerous Christian pastors, deacons and other followers of Jesus. Most of the material comes directly out of my head; I had no notes, other than what I could research at the time, and of course a good Bible. So it's conceivable I may have borrowed thoughts, ideas or concepts from sources I have forgotten or simply cannot identify. To those sources I offer my sincerest appreciation and humbly apologize for not being able to site these as references, but it would have been impossible to do so since I, myself, do not know where these thoughts had their origins.

The original purpose of this work was merely as an outlet for my frustration. I wanted to get closer to my Lord, so I started writing these pages. I did not, initially, intend it for public consumption or publication. It was to be a private journal, possibly shared with family members and close friends. I had not intended it for publication. My wife talked me into that. Originally I thought it was useful only to me, but my wife convinced me otherwise. So, this synopsis of my spiritual journey owes its existence to my lovely wife.

In many ways I've had to reinvent myself as my spiritual journey transpired. I've been the Angry Man, the Buddhist, the Agnostic...and yes, even a Homeless One. And with each new insight, every new inroad, as my comprehension of what it's meant to be a disciple of Christ increased, I've had to remake myself into a new person, and hopefully...a better Christian. So, as my own journey continues and my understanding of the Christian faith grows and develops, I have one question for Jesus: "So who am I this time, Lord?"

May the peace of God, which passes all understanding, keep your hearts and minds through Christ Jesus. Amen.

Sitting on the Porch with Jesus

Rob Strauss
May 12, 2015

Notes and Acknowledgements:

I am greatly indebted to the ministers, priests, pastors and people of God who have guided me in my spiritual journey. Special thanks goes to Pastor John Kenreich of Our Saviour Lutheran Church in Hampton Bays, NY. He is probably the person most responsible for my coming to Christ. Our talks on any number of topics have always been helpful, informative…and always left me breathless. He has helped many to come to Christ. I'm sure the Lord has a special place for him in Heaven.

I am most indebted to Jesus Christ himself, naturally. Through the years Jesus and his Father have been very patient with my meanderings of faith; always a precarious thing at best. But through prayer and the grace of God I have made it through the furnace of doubt and confusion, to come out on the other side, standing right beside Jesus. He is my Savior, he is my Lord, and he is my friend.

And finally I must acknowledge the love, support and commitment my wife, Lucy, gave me during the time I was working on this. Without her enthusiasm and faith I would never have had the courage or discipline to finish the effort. She is an amazing woman, and I am lucky to be married to her.

To the many others I am undoubtedly indebted to, I offer my most humble thanks. It's been a long road, and in many ways I'm still going down it. Hopefully I've come to a smoother, clearer portion of the path, with less stones to trip over. At the end of the path is God. I look forward to what comes after that as well.

Chapter Notes:

Chapter One -

For a more practical treatment of worrying from the Christian standpoint I would recommend: <u>Running Scared: Fear, Worry, and the God of Rest</u> by Edward T. Welch - New Growth Press (October 2007).

There are dozens of books and other sources available about life in ancient times, and some excellent children's encyclopedic books with illustrations that colorfully show how people lived in ancient times.

Chapter Two –

This chapter is my attempt to present the alternative point of view as far as "talking on the porch with Jesus" is concerned. Many evangelical Christians do not approve of my "lackadaisical" approach to talking to Jesus as a friend, claiming it's irreverent and disrespectful to the Deity.   I disagree, and I tried to explain why in this chapter.

Of course I strongly suggest reading the "Narnia'" books by C. S. Lewis.   They're a wonderful allegory for the Christian message.

Chapter Three –

As other topics, there are many books about managing anger in a Christian way, such as <u>When Good Men Get Angry: How to Understand and Deal with Anger in a Godly Way</u> by Bill Perkins (Tyndale House - 2009) and <u>Uprooting Anger: Destroying the Monster Within</u> by Kay W. Camenisch (Carpenters Son Publishing – 2014), which also contains an excellent eight-week Bible study sequence. But that is just one example.

Christians have been pondering the implications of "free will" for centuries, starting with St. Augustine's <u>On Free Choice of the Will</u> and <u>City of God</u>, <u>The Bondage of the Will</u> by Martin Luther, <u>Freedom of the Will</u> by Jonathan Edwards, and most of the writings of John Calvin. For a more modern treatment you might try <u>Free Will and the Christian Faith</u> by W. S. Anglin (Oxford University Press (February 1991). I'm not sure we're any closer to fully understanding free will.

Chapter Four –

We are all capable of comforting those who are grieving; it doesn't have to be arduous or awkward. I have only touched on a few concepts hoping this might help those who have trouble comforting others who have suffered grievous loss. The Bible is my main source for spiritual inspiration, with many verses offering comfort, such as John 16:33: "I have told you these things, so that in me you may have peace. In this world you will have trouble. But take heart! I have overcome the world." You can't go wrong by going to the Bible for direction and comfort.

There are also many books and publications on the subject of bereavement—too many to list here—that can be found in most bookstores and online. For more information on the topic I would recommend contacting any of the professional and non-profit agencies such as the American Grief Academy and the US Department of Veterans Affairs (for veterans and their families) which offer informational material and counseling services.

There are several bereavement support groups available (again, too many to list here) as well as more official groups for those seeking training and certification in grief and bereavement counseling, such as the group my wife belongs to: the "Stephen Ministry." This lay-ministry consists of caring people who have gone through the rigorous "Stephen Series" training to "…provide one-to-one Christian care to hurting people in and around the congregation." For more information on this and other caring resources please see: https://www.stephenministries.org/

Chapter Five –

My main motivation in writing this chapter was to show that Christians are very aware of the counter-arguments presented by humanists, atheists and agnostics. We read too. There is a multitude of literature on the subject of myths and how they relate, or do not relate, to the New Testament narratives, and it's easy to get bogged down. If taken as a whole the balance is just about equal as to which "side" wins the argument. But honestly…there's no argument, no winner or loser. There are only questions…and an overabundance of alleged answers. Ultimately what you believe is a matter of faith, and due in a large part to the culture you were born into.

The so called "debunking" of Christianity is popular these days, and the literature is awash with critics who delight in pointing out the parallels in pagan mythology. Likewise there is an equal abundance of literature, running the gamut of serious apologetics to popular inspirational pamphlets, supporting the veracity of the Gospel narratives and the rest of the New Testament. You have to ensure the equanimity of the information you receive; you don't want to settle for just one side of the story. But don't take my word for it, see for yourself. Read about the old myths and then re-read the New Testament (or read it for the first time if you haven't yet) and see what honestly strikes you as Truth, with a capital "T." You don't have to turn off your brain, but don't turn off your heart either.

Chapter Six –

It's a cliché, but it's true: charity does begin at home. More specifically in your home church or parish. Try to give generously to the local charities of your choice, especially the ones who care for those less fortunate, such as "Mana on Main Street" (http://mannaonmain.org/) mentioned in this chapter.

Chapter Seven –

True story: My wife and I really did receive an excommunication notice in the mail from the first church we joined as a couple. It made a lasting impression on us.

As mentioned in the chapter, I truly believe a well-organized church shouldn't need to require specific amounts of money from its members. And many churches do not do this. They also do not (contrary to popular belief) pressure their congregation for money. Having served on several church boards, and presided over one for several years, I know it's difficult but possible to come up with a practical church budget without requiring tithes or specific donations from members. Of course my experience is only with small to moderate-size churches. I cannot speak to the needs of large and mega-churches, which I'm sure are various and different. I only question the <u>need</u> for mega-churches.

Concerning the word "<u>agápe</u>," the Greek language as used by Paul and other New Testament writers denotes four distinct types of "love": <u>agápe</u>, <u>éros</u>, <u>philía</u>, and <u>storgē</u>. You had to distinguish the different types of "love" from the context. The word <u>éros</u> is familiar to us from words such as <u>erotic</u>, and means sexual passion. <u>Philía</u> is used to mean "friendship" or "affectionate regard" and should also be familiar from Philadelphia: the "city of brotherly love." <u>Storgē</u> is what we might call "familial love" or "parental love": the love mothers and fathers feel for their children, and <u>visa versa</u>. As stated in the text, <u>agápe</u> means a "selfless, sacrificial, unconditional love" that is often translated as "charity" in the King James Version of the Bible.

Chapter Eight –

The "Toddler's Ten Commandments" is a popular list that circulates on the Internet, with no actual author associated with it. It is also called the "Dog Property Laws" sometimes.

Chapter Nine –

Regarding truth, your best bet for a primary source is the Bible. That's truth with a capital "T."

For a good explanation of "relativism" (the belief that truth is relative and nothing can be really known) I'd recommend: <u>True Truth: Defending Absolute Truth in a Relativistic World</u> by Art Lindsley (Inter-Varsity Press, 2004).

Perhaps the most influential writer and speaker of the 20th century on Buddhism, and one of my favorite authors/philosophers, was Alan Watts. I have read many of his books (most of which are still in publication) and listened to many of his lectures (which are available on the web), and always found him informative and entertaining. In fact he described himself as a "philosophical entertainer."

Another of Mr. Watts' more readable books on Buddhism are: The Way of Zen (Pantheon; First US Edition 1957) and Behold the Spirit: A Study in the Necessity of Mystical Religion (Pantheon Books, 1971).

I recently discovered that Alan Watts died in 1973 of complications due to alcoholism. I was shocked to hear this. But as I pondered this disturbing fact I came to understand that perhaps the eastern religions such as Hinduism and Buddhism do not really offer much support for those suffering from an addiction such as alcoholism. Buddhism and Taoism are largely nontheistic, and so there is no deity to pray to for strength and support. Hinduism, with its caste system and class hierarchy, supports the status quo and encourages its adherents to live with the "hand they were dealt"; it does not foster self-improvement or personal problem-solving. As a matter of fact I read an article on the death of Alan Watts that suggested being an alcoholic was perfectly compatible with Taoism because, after all, your spiritual path is your responsibility. After reading that, I was very happy to have a personal God I can look to for strength and inspiration.

Chapter Ten –

The anecdote of the buzzard, the bat and the bumblebee is another of those online items that makes the rounds every now and then, author unknown.

The platitude: "Any problem that can be solved with money is not really a problem" has been known to grandparents and the rooms of AA for decades, perhaps longer. It's a lesson that's hard to learn. But we really need to learn it.

For further ideas about our culture's fondness for money and riches, and how we put personal wealth ahead of God, I would recommend two books by Brian McLaren: A Generous

<u>Orthodoxy</u> (Zondervan/Youth Specialties, 2004) and <u>The Church on the Other Side</u> (Jossey-Bass, 2001).

Chapter Eleven –

The story of the "Cracked Pot" is also one of those online items that circulates from time to time with an anonymous author. It appears on many web sites, including one for Joyce Meyer. My own research has seen it attributed to Sacinandana Swami. I am indebted to whoever came up with the story, for it is a beautiful illustration of how God uses all of us, despite our flaws.

Chapter Twelve –

I knew I couldn't ignore the homosexual issue, but I did not want to delve too deeply into the topic since it is still a sticky question. What I present here in this chapter is basically the general Christian viewpoint on sin and tolerance. I know nothing has been resolved; I didn't try to resolve anything. I only wanted to get the issue out there to examine Christian tolerance in general. There are many differing points of view in the Christian church on this topic, and I do not claim to represent any one group. In this chapter I have only outlined my <u>own</u> understanding of this challenging subject.

There are a multitude of good books out there on Christian tolerance. One of the better ones, although a bit dated now, is: <u>Christianity, Social Tolerance and Homosexuality: Gay People in Western Europe from the Beginning of the Christian Era to the 14th Century</u> by John Boswell (University of Chicago Press, 1980). For those interested in the "pro-gay" side of the debate I would recommend: <u>God and the Gay Christian: The Biblical Case in Support of Same-Sex Relationships</u> by Matthew Vines (Convergent Books, 2014). Although I do not share the same views as Mr. Vines, who is admittedly gay, it is an interesting treatment of the few references in the Bible to same-sex behavior.

Chapter Thirteen –

There is a lot of negative literature out there that is critical of Christians celebrating Halloween. One example is: <u>The Facts on Halloween</u> by the writing team of John Ankerberg, John Weldon, and Dillon Burroughs (Harvest House Publishers, 2008). Strangely, I have not come across many good books supporting the celebration of Halloween; most of the Christian literature is critical toward it. I did find a pamphlet available on Amazon.com entitled: <u>Christian Origins of Halloween</u> by Angie Mosteller, director of a non-profit educational organization dedicated to teaching the Christian history of holidays (Rose Publishing, 2012) that presents a fairer treatment of Halloween in my opinion.

But basically, the only power Halloween has over you is what you let it have. If you're having trouble with your faith, or feel uneasy about Halloween, then please, do not participate in the celebration. But if you don't buy into the criticisms and feel comfortable celebrating the harmless holiday, then I don't think there's anything wrong with having fun by wearing costumes and letting kids trick or treat.

I have purposely not mentioned Wicca (the modern-day term for the pagan witchcraft religion), as I did not want to confuse the issue. I'm sure anyone interested in further information can find a plethora of literature on the subject at most bookstores and online.

For a further look into the pagan influences in Christianity I would recommend: <u>Paganism in Our Christianity</u> by Arthur Weigall (Kessinger Publishing, LLC, 2010).

Chapter Fourteen –

For more descriptions of the beauty of the Bible see: <u>A New Kind of Christian: A Tale of Two Friends on a Spiritual Journey</u> (Jossey-Bass, 2001) by Brian McLaren as well as a book already mentioned: <u>A Generous Orthodoxy</u> (Zondervan/Youth Specialties, 2004).

Chapter Fifteen –

For more on Christians as teachers see: <u>More Ready than You Realize: The Power of Everyday Conversations</u> by Brian McLaren (Zondervan, 2002).

Chapter Sixteen –

Many fellow "baby boomers" and members of my generation have a tradition of listening to Arlo Guthrie's 18-minute folk classic "Alice's Restaurant Massacree" (aka "Alice's Restaurant") on Thanksgiving Day. The song is really not about Thanksgiving (more about stupidity really), but it has become a tradition and I have held fast to it through the decades. The song was popular in the late 60s and there was even a movie made starring Guthrie as himself. Since then it has become a regular feature of Thanksgiving Day, being broadcasted at noon on radio stations across the country, bringing multiple generations of listeners together in fun and laughter.

Chapter Seventeen –

After Mel Gibson's move "The Passion of Christ" came out people were very interested in precisely why Jesus had to suffer so and die in the way shown in the movie (which even for New Testament times during the Roman Empire was a bit exaggerated). One book that came out trying to explain the reasons why Jesus had to die for us was: <u>The Passion of Jesus Christ: 50 Reason Why He Came to Die</u> by John Piper (Crossway Books, 2004). This book is excellent because it presents the reasons in simple language using plenty of Bible references in short, readable chapters.

In the New Testament Jesus knew he was headed for the cross. But in my opinion, after reading the biblical accounts, I do not believe he fully understood why, exactly, he had to suffer and die. As a man, and at the time, I think he went to the cross based solely on the faith he had in his Father. The redemption theology came later.

There is an overabundance of books about the "End of Days" (especially after the year 2000) and movies as well, but if you really want to know anything about the "Second Coming of Christ" I would stick to the New Testament, in verses such as 2 Timothy 3:1-5 and 1 Thessalonians 4:13-18…and especially the Book of Revelation. Outside of the Bible things get a bit jumbled and misleading.

For a more thorough treatment of the topic of angels and Christianity I recommend: <u>What the Bible Says about Angels</u> by Dr. David Jeremiah (Multnomah Books, 1996).

For more on a "new kind of evangelism" see Brian McLaren's book <u>More Ready than You Realize: The Power of Everyday Conversations</u> (Zondervan, 2002) already cited in the notes for Chapter Fifteen.

I realize the views expressed in this chapter represent what some might call "theological liberalism" or "post-modernism," but I disagree. I do not believe that Christian doctrine is "evolving" as some post-modernists insist, but rather our understanding of it is developing as we come to new revelations from the scriptures. Is it "theological liberalism" to keep the emphasis on love and forgiveness? Many critics of the kinder, gentler approach contend it's not assertive enough and dissipates the importance of the cross, denying Jesus Christ is the only way to the Father. I don't believe it dissipates or denies any of that. But at the same time…does it mean all other religions are completely invalid, including other denominations <u>within Christianity</u>? I find this equally hard to accept, and I know there are many like-minded folks. Christ <u>is</u> the only way. The New Testament makes that pretty plain. But how do we communicate the Good News so that it sounds like <u>good news</u>? I would say by keeping the emphasis on God's love, on forgiveness and service to others. This is the way Christianity differs from other religions: in our love for each other and our fellow sinners. The followers of Islam, for example, also insist their way is the only way. Militant Muslims (note: <u>not</u> mainstream Muslims, but the militant minority) believe that by killing infidels they will ensure their place in the afterlife, in Heaven. By contrast, Jesus tells us to love our enemies. That's quite a difference. Our way is not the world's way. It's God way.

Chapter Eighteen –

For more on Christian hope, or for anyone experiencing hopelessness I highly recommend: <u>For The Tough Times: Reaching Toward Heaven for Hope</u> by Max Lucado (Thomas Nelson Publishers, 2008). The book was written as a response to the events of September 11, 2001 and touches on the hopelessness many of us experience at the injustice of the world, the death of a loved one or the aftermath of a broken relationship.

Chapter Nineteen –

The verse from the Book of Numbers (Numbers 6:24–26) in the Old Testament is the oldest biblical text outside the Bible ever found, and the oldest known extra-biblical reference to the God of Israel.

Chapter Twenty –

Merry Christmas!!

Rob Strauss